I'm Still Here

I'm Still Here

Charlene McRae

CONTENTS

CHAPTER

1

In the beginning – 1

Please she pleaded knowing what was about to happen, she fell against the wall with her arms up in a pleading position. But her pleas went unheard and after the third or fourth hit with the bat she was numb. She stopped pleading for her life and for some reason she started to think about her life when she was younger maybe around eleven or twelve years old. She saw herself outside in the bright sunshine playing in the snow with her friends. She was the happiest child growing up, raised in a great neighborhood with both her parents. But something went terribly wrong. How did she end up here on the floor being beaten half to death over some crack cocaine. Then she drifted back in time back to that sunny day in the snow.

(Get ready to take a journey and look through the eyes of Rosalind. Her life goes from bad to worst but there is one thing for sure and she will tell you herself. No matter what I have been through because of God's Grace. I'm Still Here!! Fasten your seat belt this ride is going to get a little bumpy).

Come on you'll we got to make this fort before they come and kill us with snow balls Rosalind said. She was making as many snow balls as fast as she could all the girls knew that she made the hardest snow balls out of all of them. Hey wait a minute we need more time Rosalind yelled at the boys as they tried to do a sneak attack. They were so busy trying to finish the fort that they did not see what was about to happen to them. It had to be around 20 boys standing there with big smiles on their faces with runny noses. They were all holding so many snow balls it was not funny. They looked at Rosalind and said hey girl you got a lot of snow balls down there and you saying you need more time you girls always need more time. Hello what do you expect we are girls what do you think. They all turned around as though they were going to give us more time. You know how boys are so I ask yourself did we get more time… of course not!

There we were again in the hallway taking off hats, gloves, boots and coats because of course we got our butts kicked but we did not care it was part of the fun. There was always a few girls that got mad and started crying and saying I don't want to play they hit too hard. They hit me in my face that's not fair. After that the boys would tease the ones who were soft they would pretend to be girls and throw snowballs like a girl and run off screaming like a girl. That would even get them really man go figure.

Growing up in the projects in the Canarsie section of Brooklyn was really great. In the early 60's there were a lot of Italian's living there very few black families lived in that section at that time. But there was no color thing going on in our neighborhood like it was in some other places. Most of my best friends were Italian but my two best friends were Maryann and Theresa. We had what you would call courts and in each there were four buildings very nice the ones I lived in were only three stories high. Nice grass with chains going around them and you were not allowed to walk on the grass and we had nice beds of flowers in the center. You better not get caught walking on that grass because if you did your parents had to pay a fine. If your parent had to pay a fine everyone knew what family it was that had to pay too. Right across the street we had a beautiful park and a big baseball field. We would have picnics in the grass cook outs. We played a lot of games there the whole court would be outside and playing. Punch ball and baseball but the best was in the summer when we would get our skates and play roller derby. In the winter we would make all butterfly

Angels in there, back in the day it Canarsie was the bomb as they use to say.

Can you bring out your bike Rosalind? Maryann asked because everyone had out their bikes out that day. I have to ask my mother and I kind of knew how that would go she always gave me a speech before I came outside. Listen to me little girl you go outside do not get out there and start calling me from the window because I don't want to hear it and don't have your little friends asking for you. I never listened so of course I went and called her from the window to ask if I can get my bike. You know I had to have my friends next to me thinking that would help her to say yes if they start begging with me. She took a long time to come to the window and the first thing she says what did I tell you before you went outside? Well I did not get the right answer but at least she did not tell me to come upstairs. Before I could say anything she would say and don't start mumbling either. Yes mam I said as I turned around to walk away from under the window. How did she do that she always did that it's like she knows what I was going to do before I did it. You can ride with me Maryann said and I was ready to go so I got on the back of her bike. She was a great bike rider like me and I got on the back of her bike we always road on one another's bike. We were riding fast back to the court to see who would be the first and who would be the last. We were coming around the curve so fast and trying not to crash but it was too late. We started laughing as we got up off the ground and as I was wiping my hands on my clothes and looked at them my whole palm was open. Everybody stopped laughing and saw all the blood and meat hanging out of my hand my mother heard my mouth and came running downstairs. Wow I got stitches inside and out with a cast on and I knew I was bad the first one in the court to have a cast on. That was a big deal back then all the parents were so nice to me and my parents were too. Everyone wanted to know how it felt did it hurt when they did it all those kinds of questions and of course I said no.

That would be the first of many scars to come.....

We had two bedrooms but now that mommy is having another baby we needed more rooms. So we moved right to the next building from the 2nd floor now living on the 3rd floor. Why you always touching my stuff the girl said sounding like a white girl which is my sister Ann. Scream again and I am going to punch you dead in your face I said. I am really going to go and tell mommy now. So off she went screaming like one of those white girls in the movies and I knew what was going to be next. Come here right now ok mommy but mommy let me and I would get cut off. Don't say another word when I speak you listen. Ok but mommy can you listen to me and the next thing I knew I was getting hit in the back of my head by my dad. Where did he come from I didn't even know he was I the house. My dad who stood about 6-5 very nice built and handsome if I must say so myself and after that smack I did not make another sound. I marched in my room while mumbling very low under my breath. I heard that my mother said. How did she hear that she always does that she must have bionic ears or something? Oh and for the record I have only one sister and one brother.

I only wish she could hear what was really going on deep down inside....

Raised in the Church you wouldn't think so but I was. Let's see I was on the Usher Board and the Choir. I did not want to go but I had to go but when I think back it was not all that bad. The young people in our Church were cool but the elders of course they did not understand us young folk. Then there was Rev. Williams I loved him he was so kind and I will say that he was really a man of God. You can't say that today about these so called pastors. It's time for us to do our march. Ok watch out because when I marched I marched. All the elders would say go head girl you doing that march step on. After Church Rev would come to me and say now child you know its ok for you to march but, you putting just a little bit more in your step take it easy remember you in God's house. Yes Rev. Williams I would reply but yeah you're right of course I did not stop.

I think in his own way he was trying to warn me even at my young age that I had to be very careful because Satan was a very busy person and I would soon find out just how busy he was.....

CHAPTER

2

The First Signs of Pain

Yeah that's what I'm talking about school is out and my sister and I are headed to Harlem in the Lincoln Projects on 135th street and Park Ave. My Auntie Mary and my cousins lived there I mean my cousins were the shit I mean that in every sense of the word. Before coming to Harlem we used to go down south to be with my grandmother from my father's side. I did not like her much she was mean I guess that is the way they were but I didn't care I did not like her or going down there. We used to pick cotton and walk barefoot down the road. There was even an outhouse that we had to use. Horrible with all the bugs crawling and the smell was unbelievable. We had a cousin that had a little hole in the wall club use to be in his house called the red light I guess because there was a red light outside, with all the bugs hitting it. I mean terrible I would go home with my hair matted to my head because my grandmother did not know how to do hair. I begged my mother not to let me go but every summer the station wagon would come and we would have our bags and some food to eat on the way down.

Harlem was it I mean I could not wait to get there for those two months better than nothing at all. I had so much fun with all the friends that I had met and we always hook back up and pick up where we left off. I had my boyfriend there and when my Aunt found out she cursed him out so bad that it was over before it began. She said he was too old for me and that I had no business seeing him, of course she knew him and his family. My sister had a boyfriend too he was cool but I was mad I could not have one so why should she have one no fair not fair. If you don't know that everyplace except Brooklyn would know all the dances before them they was the last one to know. I knew all of them when I came home from Harlem I use to show off my new moves and of course I was able to dance and I was very good. My parents would have company over and they would be playing music and my father would always call me to come and dance. He would say she is crazy as hell but she can dance her ass off watch her and then he would say go girl and would try to dance with me. Those are one of the few good times I remember having with my dad. Harlem was the places to be all the friends I made and they had some fly guys in Harlem I mean dam they were fine. All that was fun great times with my cousins and my Aunt I really miss that. It was good until we found out that my Aunt was very sick and we went to see her it was hard. It was even harder when she passed away it's like I could not understand that why did she have to die and leave us. I missed her so much I mean I never cried so much in my life like I did when my Aunt died. Things were never the same and I did not want to go back over there after she dies it's like I would go to the bathroom and look at her bed and cry all over again. Soon after that my cousins all got married and moved out and still to this day I have one cousin that still lives there in that same apartment.

My father used to say that I was crazy and we never got along it's like he could not stand me and I could not stand him and I mean at all. Where is the love and I am not talking about the song either. I cannot explain it not even now not if I wanted to I really don't understand what happened to the love. It's funny how life goes and you never know what is going to happen next. How does someone at such an early age go through something so horrendous that you cannot begin to explain? Well that's what happened to me and I cannot explain it to this day. Depression for what I mean I was just a child sixteen what the hell happened I cannot begin to tell you why. One day I was home alone and I was feeling depressed and I don't know what happened I began slashing my wrist with a knife and crying at the same time. What the hell are you doing are you trying to kill yourself but just put it down and call someone now. Am I glad that I stopped when I did yes I am if not I would not be able to tell my story. Sad I guess you can say that was a sign and I had no one around that could see the signs so I went under the radar undetected. The blood was there and so were the tears what I did not know that even that early in my life not matter what I was going through He was there even then. It was not so bad that I had to go to the hospital but I called my best friend Maryann who lived right downstairs from me on the second floor. Her mom was like my second mom I loved her so much she made me come downstairs and she bandaged my wrist. My mother was very upset she started crying and asking me why he did that what was wrong with me. What is the problem did I do something to you why would you do that? I did not have an answer for her not at all I had any idea why I went that route instead of talking to my friends. My father could not care less if would have accomplished what I set out to do or was I what he always called me crazy. We didn't talk about it after that it was as though the whole thing never happened. Rev. Washington came and prayed for me. But I know as much as I loved him, his prayers would go unheard for what would seem like forever.

My sister and I did not get along and I mean that in every sense of the word I could not stand her and she did not care too much for me either. She was my sister but we were like night and day. We had a curfew and of course missy goodie two shoes would always keep hers but me I never kept mine. If my parents told her to do something she did just what they said but tell me to do something you better believe that I did just the opposite. I had a thing about rules and you know that if you don't follow the rules things are bound to go wrong very wrong. But I was young and why do I need rules I made my own rules. As long as you're living under my roof you will do what I say. And I knew it would not be long before I got fed up with the rules. You think you know everything you got it all figured out. My way turned out not so good and it all happened so fast.

High school what a big difference then JHS you feel a little more mature then you did last year. I attended HS school for all girls and I was going to be a nurse that was my major so I thought. After my first year of high school I changed that tune quick too much blood for me although I would see a lot of my own in the years to come. I know I had to have three years of my vocational studies in order to graduate. My counselor told me that if I did well and maintained a high average that will be the only way I would graduate on time. Well guess what I maintained an average of 98 my grades were so good that when I got to my senior year I was in the co-op program. That is a program you was allowed to be picked for where you went to work in the field you chose and went to school for 2 weeks wait and got paid too. I worked in Manhattan at an insurance company. You could not tell me nothing I was on top of the world no problems what so ever. Getting excellent grades meeting new people everything was great. One weekend I wanted to go bowling with my friends so I asked my mother and of course she in return said go ask your father. Daddy can I go bowling with my friends? No you are not leaving this house so go back in your room. What why can't I go what did I do its right across the street what do you mean I cannot go why are you doing this? Who you talking to you better shut up and get your ass in that room. I stormed out the bedroom and went into my bedroom and started pulling my clothes out of the drawer and crying at the same time. There was no reason he told me I could not go across the street to the bowling alley I had done nothing wrong. What are you doing why are you taking out all your clothes. I am leaving I am not going to stay here I hate him I don't like him. My sister is looking at me like what the hell happened to you because you can't go bowling so you're leaving. Where are you going to go and where will you live my sister asked me. Mind your business and don't ask me any questions, don't worry about where I am going. I loved my mother but I cannot live with him anymore he is getting on my nerves. I did not go anywhere I stayed home but I put some clothes in a bag and wrote my mother a long letter. I went to work the next morning and I left the letter on the table I knew that my mother would find it. My mother called me screaming and crying at work asking me what is wrong, why are you leaving. She was going to make me start crying is she did not stop so I told her I love her please stop crying. You know how your father is so don't do that he loves you he just has his ways that's all please come home. We are both crying and I told her I love you mommy and I hung up the phone. Maryann called me and said what is wrong with you what happened is this about the bowling last night? You are not going to do anything stupid are you please let me come and meet you after work. I am not going to do anything stupid so don't worry about that and you don't have to come here. Listen I am coming and you better not leave me either I will be there when you get off I will meet you in the lobby.

Let's go Maryann said when I came off the elevator and her and my other best friend, is standing there waiting. I am not going home, not yet anyway. So we went to Flatbush to our other friend's house. We played some music acted crazy and talked we always had a good time when we went over there. She had a brother I thought he was so cute and I did not know how to act when he was in the room. He knew it and he was older than I was I never had a boyfriend I was only 17. Ok let's go it's getting late and her brother drove us home in his car yeah he was too old for me for sure. I got home and I walked in the door and my sister is there with her boyfriend sitting in the living room. Where have you been she yelled? Shut up and mind your business don't worry about where I been. Where is mommy I asked my sister and before I could even get out the question she yells you are in trouble. Everyone is here looking for you, daddy and mommy and even grandpa came out here from Long Island. Grandpa is not here your lying I know he did not come all the way over here to look for me. When mommy called and she was crying and told him that you ran away he came over here quick. Then I thought to myself she must have told him that I tried to kill myself too and that is why he came over not knowing what I was going to do. I loved my grandpa so much he was unable to walk he had to be driven everywhere he wanted to go he was my world. He is going to kill me when he sees me and daddy is looking for me I don't believe that one he is the reason that I was going to run away in the first place. Well maybe you can go down stairs and tell them that you're here they just pulled up. I got downstairs and my father saw me coming across the street he got out the car and walked the other way. My mom was crying and I got in the car and my mom asked me if I was ok. She told me she did not care what my father did, don't do that again he loves you or he would not have been out here looking for you. Hi grandpa and I gave him a kiss on his cheek and he said what's going on monkey that is what he called me. Nothing daddy won't let me do anything I asked to go across the street I don't know why grandpa. That's your daddy that's just the way he is but you can't go doing stuff like that get me all worried. I am sorry grandpa and I am sorry to you too mommy and you too Grandma Rose. So we sat and talked for a while and then I went on upstairs and my grandpa went home. After my little episode every time I wanted to go someplace I was able to go no questions asked. My dad didn't change though because that little bit of freedom I had did not last long it was back to business as usual.

June 1970 Graduation great day finally I am on my way to college and I graduated with good grades I was looking good too. I had it all figured out college good job can afford a really nice place of my own. September I was starting and only 17 years old I thought I was the shit working still until it was time for me to start college. Marketing Management is what I majored in I wanted to have my own business or be able to run someone else's company. I had my grants to pay for college and my work schedule so when I was not in class I was working. Worked at an elementary school and then at the Psychiatric ward at a hospital not knowing that one day I would be a patient in that same hospital.

Still going to Church and that Sunday we had to stay because we had to sing for an afternoon service. This time I was going to Church because I wanted to not because I had too. Standing outside me and some other girls and a little green car passed by and I said he is cute in that little car and he smiled and I did also. Then the car slowed down and backed up and I got a little nervous and he signaled for me to come to the car and I said no you come here. And he backed up some more and I think I had a heart attack. You go to this Church he asked me and I said yeah this is my Church. He gave me his number and I gave him mine and he started calling me and inviting me to come out with him but I was afraid. The first time I said that he can come over to my house my mother did not like him. She told me that he was too old for me and that I should not be seeing him. He use to come and pick me up from work and I would go to his house and listen to music he was trying to get me to have sex with him. I said hell no I am not going to have sex with him I was afraid number one and I was still a virgin and thinking like my father and mother had me thinking. He smoked a lot of weed all the time I was with him in his apartment that's all he did. I can't talk much I use to do it to but with my girls not outside with people I don't know. It's was cool then we knew each other well we grew up together and we had fun when we smoked laughing at one another all the time while listening to music. One night I was smoking with my friends at Theresa's house because that is where we always smoked at. And we had our first party at her house too we had so much fun there and we even cooked food for the morning folks. One day we was smoking and we were listening to Aretha Franklin bridge over troubled waters and I saw or what I thought I saw was Aretha walking on the album I quit. One night I was with my friend and I smoked a bag of weed just to get my head ready for what I was about to do with him.

When I got home that night I saw my girlfriends outside sitting across the street in the park and they asked me of course the big question. Come here and tell us all about it I know you did something don't play with me look at you cannot stop smiling. Well yeah I did something but I have to be honest with you I don't remember if it was good or not. That is bad my first time I should feel great and different but I don't and that is sad. See he was not the one even though he was your first he was not the one if he did not make you feel that way. I know he was not the one and I don't think I even want to see him again after tonight. What are you going to tell him when he wants to see you again or call you it might not have been good to you but I know he is going to want some more he took your virginity. I don't care I don't want to see him and that is what I am going to tell him when he calls me. I think I kind of hinted to him tonight that I did not want to see him again. I am sorry to hear that I thought we were going to get the scoop on the whole sex thing and first time but I guess not. They say that is supposed to be the best sex ever the first time that's how they make it seem. It probably would have been if I would have been with the right persona and I did not have to get high first. Well the right person can be my first time ever I really want that more than anything right now he was not the right person. Just as that experience faded away so did he if you notice I did not even mention a name?

The sad part is that I have not yet found the right person to say that when I was with them the first time it was special. Sad part of my life I must say, but what can you do where is he? Still looking....

College much different than HS I mean you had professors and classes were different just the atmosphere was great really felt like a real adult. I met new friends and they were really cool nothing like when I was growing up in Canarsie. In my major class there was a guy name Reggie and boy was he handsome I mean really cute and you could say I had a little crush on him ok really big crush on him. I knew a guy like that would never talk to me I mean he said hi and everything but that was it. I had a friend I use to hang out with his name was Rodney and I we were in the cafeteria one day and I told him about Reggie and I said he thought he was too cute and a little stuck up. Why do you say that I know him that's my friend we live in the same neighborhood? He is not like that really he is a great guy. Yeah whatever you say and you say he is cool yeah he is the girls go crazy over him. Do you want to meet him I can introduce you and I said no don't do that I don't want to meet him. I don't believe you but ok but don't talk about him if you don't want to meet him at least and see what kind of guy he is. I will talk to you later I have to get to class and work after that. Ok Rosalind I will talk to you later sure you don't want to meet him? I am sure I don't want to meet him so stop asking me that. I see the way you smile when you talk about him I don't think you mean that. You better not say anything to him about me Rodney doesn't do that please. The next day I am walking in the hall going to my class and someone behind me said so you think I am stuck up really? I turned around and said who are you talking to? You it's you that I am talking to someone told me that you said that about me and it's not true. I am going to kill Rodney. So you did say that or else how would you know that it was Rodney who told me that? I said it yes I did so what that is the way it looks to me. We are in the same class and I always speak to you but you act like you don't want to talk or something you're the one who is stuck up. I don't think so I have to go to class now ok Rosalind I will see you in class this is not over. Listen I don't want any problems with your girlfriend see us talking I am sure she will be jealous. That might be true if I had a girlfriend I am sure she would be jealous of you. I smiled I must have showed every tooth I had in my mouth the biggest blush ever. Right I will see you later I don't want to be late for class messing with you. Rosalind don't forget this conversation will be continued. I walked away and my heart was beating so fast I could hardly breathe I could not believe he said those things to me. Calm down Rosalind he is just a guy nothing to have a heart attack over.

Well you guessed it right after that encounter it was Reggie and Rosalind from that day on. I was so happy he was so loving and affectionate that I don't have one bad thing to say about him. He was perfect in every way nothing to complain about not one single thing he was perfect. He lived in Queens and my mother loved him he was wonderful we use to hang out he would come over for dinner. I was in heaven I never felt love until I met Reggie I did not know what love was until I met him and I will always be thankful to him for showing me what love was like. Thank you Reggie I loved you more than you will ever know I would melt in his arms when he held me. When he kissed me I felt like I was going to pass out he had perfect everything lips I mean when I think about him now I still get that same feeling. So what happened to us I asked myself a thousand times why I was so stupid how do you lose a love like that? The events that followed will change my life forever and I do mean forever. Reggie if you were to ever read this after 44 years I still feel the same way about you now that I did then would love to see you again.

One year is all I had with Reggie he transferred to another college out of town and my whole life went to hell after that. We would talk on the phone and I stopped going to college after that and went to work. He would come home and I would see him it was not the same then I mean I guess I need him to be there physically with me because once he was gone I knew we would not be the same. While he was gone I met this well did not know it then but the father of my daughter and we messed around here and there. Reggie would still come and see me when he was home but not as often sometimes I would not see him at all and the phone calls got less like his visits. Reggie came over one summer day and well I was pregnant and I did not know how to tell him that so I didn't, I thought there was a chance for us but I knew now that it was not. He will not be willing to raise another man's child and the worst part is we never had sex so I know that would have hurt him a lot so I never told him. Oh God why did this have to happen this is a man that I love to death and would do anything to be with him but I was so ashamed to even look him in the face. He knew something was wrong with me I was not showing a lot a little bump but I could not tell him. Now how did I meet this guy that I got pregnant by I will not mention his name at all. My cousin came from the south to stay with us and I got her a job working where I was when I was in HS and before I went to college. She in return met this guy and I would go with her to see him at a friend's house. That is how we met and of course when they could not find her I was the one that got in trouble because I knew where she was. Well he did not treat her so good and after a while and she got pregnant so her brothers came and got her and took that ass back down south never to return again.

When I say at the wrong place at the wrong time I know just what that means. Some people my cousin met I wish I would have never met. There was a lady that I met she was very nice and I would come over and we would hang out with the guys she became like a sister to me. Her son I loved him like my own, he was great and she was also my daughters God Mother Lorraine. My cousin's boyfriend had a sister and her name was the same as mine and we became close and there I met my daughters father there is not much more to tell then that once I got pregnant of course he did not know me. See you have to understand I had not one in my corner to help me or that I could talk to family wise. My brother was younger than I was and my sister we didn't speak half the time so when things would happen I was alone in everything. To make a long story short I met the man I met after having sex with him one time I was pregnant believe that. I did not either but that's the way it went and I know I could have had an abortion and go on with my life but I could not. And as sweet as he was when we met when I told him I was having his baby he told said the usual it isn't mine. Ok it's not yours well let me say this after I have this baby and I see you anywhere no matter where it is you better not say anything to me or my child. I cannot believe how big I was I mean it looked like I was having triplets instead of one child that is how big she was. My best friends gave me a baby shower and it was great. My first and only baby shower that day I really felt love. My mother was pissed off at me said that she was not going to help me or anything with the baby. But of course she came around and started bringing home a lot of stuff for the baby. Of course everyone that came was on my side of the family because he was not invited and I never spoke to him. It was strange though that was the second time I felt love we know when the first time was.

How are you I turned to see a cop walking next to me and I said fine and thought to myself I know he see this big stomach and he cannot be trying to holler at a sista. He was a housing cop and yes he was hitting on me a much older guy and handsome if I must say so myself. I know you can see that I am pregnant so why are you talking to me. I see that you're pregnant and I think your husband must be very happy. What he is really trying to talk to me so we talked. He was very nice always came around my mother thought he was nice I thought he must like pregnant pussy a lot. And yes he did but he was also controlling and that I was not with. Always brought me food and gave me money whatever I needed all I had to do was ask and I got it. When it was time for me to go to the hospital my mother called him and he took me in the car with sirens going off. I gave birth to a 9lb.8oz baby girl she was too big for my little butt. He came to the hospital every day and when I got home he had bought so much stuff and gave me money to make sure I did not want for anything. Ok the moment I have been waiting for the baby is here now he wants to buy me a co-op so he can have total control over me now. My mother was mad with me when I told him hell no, I don't want to live in a place that you are paying for so you can control me. Well when that did not work out he felt that he no longer wanted to see me, I rejected him and he did not like it. Oops too bad that is not happening not now or ever. Short lived relationship with a cop good while it lasted but was nothing I was looking for I am no longer pregnant why would

I need an ole' man literally speaking. My daughter's name well let's say I had nothing to do with it my best friends gave her the first and middle name well of course she had my last name.

My sister got married to the organist of our Church and she was pregnant the same time I was. Our daughters are two months and one day apart I love her to death.

My daughter and I always went to see Lorraine her Godmother and she loved going over there and I had a great time. We were looking out of the window one day and this guy walks up yelling out to Lorraine. Who is that with you in the window and I looked at him and she said oh that's Ros and he said hey my name is Chuck, hi what's up I replied. He had a cousin named James and when I saw him I thought to myself umm good looking slim clothes fitting to a tee. Here is Chuck and James both trying to holla and I am feeling James for real. It did not matter though because what's going to happen is going to happen no matter what. I will forever regret the choice I made to be with James now let the tears begin. I would have been better off alone then to get caught up with James. The events that followed you may think while reading this that it is a lie and think to yourself no one could go through all that and be sane. And you're absolutely right I will never be the same.

CHAPTER

3

In the beginning - 2

I must have passed out for a second and I look at my arm and it's in a u shaped and I cannot feel anything. What the hell is going on how long was I out I could not tell all I know is that I had to get out of there quick. I tried to get up and when I did it seems like my leg folded like an accordion. My knee went to my foot it was as if my bones was gone in my leg. But I had to try to get out of here the best way could. It seemed quiet maybe they left and I should go and lock the door but they might come back. Oh God they are still here they are in the bedroom looking for something that I don't have. Man finds some gloves do you see any around here look for some. Oh no they are going to beat me so bad that I will not have much of a face left and leave no prints that are what the gloves are for. I managed to get up on one leg and open the door and hopped begging for someone to please open the door and help me but of course they did not. I don't blame them if the shoe was on the other foot I would not want to get involved either. They were afraid and did not want to get involved. I tried to get up the stairs but I could not, I could hardly move the pain was coming back somewhat. They came out my apartment and wanted my keys and I did not have any and they told me to come back inside. I begged please don't hit me anymore please I am sorry please don't kill me. Then it seemed like someone felt sorry for me and called the cops thank God. I could not believe it someone felt sorry for me and for that I am grateful.

I thought that if you called the ambulance the cops came first but not in my case they never showed up. I was still in the hallway when they came they cut my pants off and asked me if I got shot because if I did I did not feel it a baseball bat will do that to you for sure. There I go off to the hospital I am sure someone will tell my daughter where I was and what happened. The blood is coming out of my leg like a water fountain everyone was staring covering their eyes as they rolled me through the emergency room to get me to a room. Mam your bone came through your leg and I don't think the bones are attached in your left arm we are going to x-ray everything first. But you definitely needs surgery because as cast will not hold that. I had no insurance they thought I was homeless that's right people that's, how bad I looked at the time lost and forgotten that's what I became.

Hey baby how you doing and I was surprised but not really I knew when he found out what happened he would be here. That is Robert he is about 30years older than I am and heavy set. He always looks out for me and soon you will find out how much he is involved in my life. You would think after that beating I would leave the drugs alone but don't hold your breath. I will be back to this with another update in a minute, but right now we are going back to James you remember him right?

CHAPTER

4

Let the pain begin

Hi how are you as I was introduced to Chuck's wife by James as we walked in the apartment. I met his kids and wife and they were all very nice made me feel right at home. She became like a sister to me we were very close.

Bergen Street I remember that apartment will never forget it for the rest of my life. I lived there with James and my daughter. I was staying with my mother still and then one night he called me and he was very sick and asked me to catch a cab and come over there to stay with him. You know how you men act when you get sick like little boys so we went over there and it was late. This was one time I should have listened to my mother when she told me not to go and I went anyway. That is how I started living with him and after I did you talk about a change what happened to the man I met. He drank a lot would always take me and my daughter to his cousins house Chuck and would leave me there until he decided to come back. The next event would be the beginning a **LIVING HELL!!!**

It was a nice summer day so I decided to take my daughter out and go visit my mom. We got an early start so I could be home in time for James to get in. She is getting so big that is all I kept hearing from everyone that saw her. I saw the time and it was getting late when I say late I mean 4 or 5pm he got home at different times. So we headed home on the bus and when we walked in the door this is what I heard. Where the fuck you been he yelled at me. I was at my mother's house I took her to see her grandmother and grandfather. You're a fuck'n liar I called your mother's house and no one answered the phone. Before I knew it he had punched me in my face so hard that I saw stars for the first time in my life I never had anyone put their hands on me before. What is wrong with you I said after that hit and before I knew it he threw me across the bed and I hit the wall and I fell on my daughter who was still in her stroller who is now on the floor screaming. Blood flowing from my mouth and my nose and I could hardly see. Please don't hit me again I am sorry I was outside sitting on the bench talking to my friends and my mother. Why did you lie you should have told me the truth when I asked you. I am sorry I should not have lied although that is what I had to do in order not to get hit again. He never called my mother's house I got beat for nothing.

Well I could not go back outside for a while I was a mess my face was four times the size including my mouth. I had never been hit before and this was only the beginning of the abuse I would suffer from this man for the next seven years. Ok I hear what you're thinking what the hell is wrong with her. He said he loved me and that he was sorry for what he did and why did that work for me; I never had anyone tell me they loved me before simple. Along with the words I love you came the fear. I had no one to help me. So here I am with a man whose love means I will kill you and believe me he did it on more than one occasion. After the beating he was sweet again I was always over Lilly's house that is Chuck's wife name and we had a great time. As long as I was there James would not give me a second thought. Oh did I mention that when I got beat real bad that I was expecting his child. The only time he did not hit me is when I was having his child but after that it was business as usual. I had a baby boy James Jr. he loved that little boy although he hardly saw him. I was rather happy when he was not around did not have to worry about beatings.

I was depressed a lot when I was with him to the point that I did not want to live so I had some pain pills and decided to end it. I prayed for my children and I laid down on the bed next to them to die. The phone rang and at first I was not going to answer the phone but I did and it was Lilly and she says what's wrong and it took me a long time to answer and she yelled in the phone what's going on Rosalind and I told her what I did. Chuck was there so fast to check on my and the kids and of course James was no place to be found. I begged them not to tell him what I did he, would have killed me for sure.

Everyone was alcoholics they all drank his brothers his cousin his mama and grandmother. His mother did not like me at all I mean at all and that goes for my daughter too. My daughter called him daddy that is the only father she knew. James also had a daughter from his wife and she and I got along very well and she called me ma of course her mother did not like that. She would say that Theresa was her sister but her mother told her that she only had a brother from her father that she was not his and not to call her sister. True but a cruel thing to say to a little girl.

Needed more room and since I was on PA I went and got a two bedroom apartment. It was a nice day so Lilly and I went and took all the kids outside to the park and we saw an ice-cream truck so we went there. Well I don't believe this there was my daughter's father on the truck. He looked at me and I told him not to say shit to me and I turned and walked away and he came off the truck. She looks just like me I am so sorry that I doubted you there is no way I can ever deny her can I please pick her up. I don't know you acted like an ass when I told you I was pregnant like I was a trick or something now you want to be daddy. He picked her up and she looked at him like who the hell are you she would not smile at first and then she with her little fast ass want to giggle. He went back on the truck and came back with a hand full of money and told me to buy her what she needs. I had to hide the money and give it to Lilly to hold for me so he would not see or find it. Think you can bring her over to my sister's house and I said I would think about it. I brought her a couple of things and why did I do that so I was asked where did I get the money from. I told him the truth but I forgot that does not work for him and I said I saw her father and her gave me money for her. I will kill you bitch you been seeing him the whole time. The first hit I ran out the door he came after me with a knife chasing me between cars trying to stab me. Yo man what the fuck is wrong with you? Chuck thank God he was coming over at the same time I was being chased by that ass hole. He grabbed James and I do mean grabbed him and threw him against the car. Once again God looked out for me and I was thankful however he will look out for me so many more times than I can count.

One day while moving and of course he was no place to be found I was pregnant again and I was in the house with the kids and I had a miscarriage moving and carrying all that stuff and of course Chuck came and rushed me to the hospital and took the kids over his house. We always lived close to one another never too far away and I am glad about that. This was not the last pregnancy I then right after that got pregnant again and he was nice again like before but I could not see myself having another child by him. I was around 5 months and the doctor told me that I might have a problem delivering and I said no I will not because I am not going to keep the baby so I had an abortion almost died and once again God saved my life. It was wrong but I asked for forgiveness I could not continue getting beat and now having problems delivering after the miscarriage. The way he was treating me I may not live long enough to raise them I did not want to do that.

Yes I believe in God and I say this because this day will show me that God loves me and He is still in the miracle business. I don't even know what happened either I did not answer him fast enough of it was not the answer that he wanted to hear. All I know is that he hit me so hard and then I hit the bed and he jumped on me and started punching me and chocking me. The kids were crying and screaming and he pushed them out and locked the door. He continued hitting me I got up off the bed and he went in his pocket and took out his knife and was swinging at me to stab me. The kids were screaming and banging on the door and I yelled please go see about the kids so they can stop crying. He looked at me and told me to stand there and don't move he went to the door with the knife still in his hand. I cannot let him stab me to death and kill me God please forgive me and please take care of my children. I closed my eyes and ran right through the closed window from the 4th floor. All you can hear is glass breaking and falling from the window. I heard someone scream but I could not tell where the voice was coming from, I could not see from the blood that was dripping down my face. I grabbed something and I could hardly see what it was what a clothes line where did that come from I always wanted one to hand the kids clothes out when I washed. The only part of my body that was still in the window was my legs. Please don't kill me I begged him as he came to the window with the knife still in his hands. Why did you do that look at how much you're bleeding? I saw a movie Dr. Jekyll & Mr. Hyde take place right in front of me he act as though he cared his voice changed and it almost sounded like he was human. Are you ok, I heard voices but I was too busy keeping my eye on the monster in front of me? Baby are you ok look at you come inside you have glass and blood everywhere. Come take my hand my thumb was almost off and he grabbed me and pulled me inside but not before I made him put the knife down. He is going to get me inside and kill me that is what he is going to do with my children watching. He took me to the bathroom and cut on the cold water and wiped the blood from my face as I held my hand under the water. He wrapped my hand and took me in the living room and sat me on the couch where he then started pulling glass out my face and head. A knock came at the door and by the knock you can tell it's the cops. Open the door is everything ok in here open the door now. He changed just that fast and picked up the knife and put it to my throat and told me to go to the door and tell them everything is ok do not open the door. No officer everything is fine no problem one of my kids was playing and broke the glass. Then just that fast he went back to taking care of me and then he demanded that I get dressed and go to the store with him. Could you imagine he wanted me to go outside with him the way I looked and everyone in the building knew he beat the shit out of me? My face was like a basketball and one of my eyes was shut and the other one partially. Still bleeding he took me to the store to walk in front of all those people. He would not go to work after this happened he claimed that he was staying home to take care of me. I know the real reason he did that is so that I would not leave the house. A week he did not go to work or leave the house maybe to go to the store and that was it. All the time I knew in my head I could not wait for him to leave I was going to grab my kids and get the hell out of there. The day he goes back to work he asks me need anything honey before I leave. No I am ok see you later and of course once again he could not understand why I would do that out of the window thing. Oh no this is a trick he is going to stay outside somewhere and wait until he sees me come out the building and run up on me and take me back upstairs and finish the job. I thought he might even come back while I was getting the kids dressed the fear that ran through me is something I cannot explain I knew I would drop dead right there on the spot. I stood there and I looked at my children and said hell no we getting the hell out of here if I see him he will have to kill me. I got strength from somewhere and I said I will do what I have to do but I will fuck him up if he comes near me or my children.

We got outside and I looked and I did not see him my heart was beating fast. I thought I would pass out I took my children and I walked so fast down the block. Mommy my daughter called out I was walking too fast and she could not keep up. Ok Rosalind slowdown is what I told myself I just wanted to get to Chucks house and if he was there I knew we would be safe. We got upstairs and everyone is saying hi and laughing saying that I was out early. They had not seen me yet and when they did all I heard was screams and I could not stop the tears from flowing. Don't go back there and I was not I am going to call my mother and ask her to come and get us from here and take me to her house. I did not know if she would do that for me I don't know was not sure but I knew I was not going back home.

I was so afraid that he was going to come back to the house and see that I was and come looking for me. Well my mother came and got me and the kids and she was like in shock when she saw me. What happened to you how did your face and you got blood coming out of your head. Ma I jumped out the window and before that he beat me up. Please ma I don't want to go back there. You're not going in there I am I want to know who he think he is putting his hands on you like that. Let him get in my face I will kill him I want to see him say anything. She pulled up right in front of the building and told me to give her the keys. I lied and told her I lost them and he was not there anyway I begged her to leave I just want to go please mommy. She finally said ok and then we left and went to my childhood home that I missed so much. Of course my father did not want to see me come there with my problems and my children. Do I have to talk to daddy that was something I did not want to do? I was praying that I did not see anyone sitting outside and want to talk and get in my business did not want to deal with that. Home and here I am looking terrible but I was home and this is the place I grew up and I am back it felt really well. Everything still looked the same nothing is out of place as always just how my mother liked it. My mother always kept a nice house and I mean clean and you better had kept it that way. I once again got the rules put on me as to what to do and what not to do in her house. She didn't see much of James Jr so she played with them while I nursed my wounds.

I am sorry the voice said on the other end as if I did not know he was going to call. Oh really your sorry I don't want to hear that something has to be wrong with you. I am tired of getting beat on I am sick of you beating me and then saying you're sorry and then beating me again. I love you and I miss you can I at least see you? No, you cannot see me and then all you heard was a dial tone from me hanging up the phone. That felt good to hang up the phone on him to let him know I am tired of his shit and I don't need him. Time passed and he called again this time my mother answered the phone and boy did she let him have it. After that he started acting really nice and I mean really nice. Hello, I have a surprise for you can I pick you up and show you what it is please. I miss you and the kids really bad and I want us to be a family again and I promise to never put my hands on you again. The words I love you melted my heart it made me forget that I almost died not too long ago at his hands. He picked me and the kids up and we went to Coney Island and I said to him to him so why are we out here. He parked the car in from of a coop apartment building looked like duplexes and I did not understand why we were there still. We got out the car and he took out keys and we went into the building and took the elevator and went an apartment and he had keys for that as well. Who lives here and why do you have keys? He handed me the keys and said we do if you will take me back. We went inside and I looked around the bedrooms were downstairs and the kitchen, dining room and living room was upstairs and the balcony too. Yes you're right the kids and I were living in Coney Island.

Things were going good and I decided to go back to school and took up computer programming and technology and did well if I must say well better than that I did excellent. So good, that my teacher put in a recommendation for me at a company in Connecticut. I could not wait to get home and tell him the good news. Well that did not work at all and he was not happy about that and told me to go and take my daughter but I was not going to take his son with me. I cried and asked why what is wrong with you there is no money coming out of your pocket they pay for everything. I am not going there with no job and no money and have to depend on you for everything. So what's wrong with that I am sure you can get a job there they have restaurants there too. He did not want to hear that so of course I did not go I wanted both my children there with me. So you see although I know he was cheating on me he would stay out days at a time and not come home what does that mean. He had some friends that lived in the complex they were ok because of his friends wife I joined the tenants committee. That was something different and exciting we took charge of everything community center and security was out best friend.

There was a bad snow storm and he had not been home and I needed some pampers and milk so I called his job. Hi how can I help you and I told her my name and I was looking for James and she greeted me with such a warm welcome made me think I knew her. Then she said that she was sorry about James how is he doing. What do you mean sorry to hear about James I don't know what happened to him. Then she told me about the accident he was in and he was in the hospital. I could have acted as though I was upset but I was not but I put on a little show. I will come over and bring you what you need are you sure that's it. Yes I am sure and you don't have to do that with this weather I want to thank you so much I really appreciate you doing that. She was a white girl and she did not have to do that so made me wonder is this someone he was messing with had to be for her to go out her way. We had a bad snow storm and there was no way I was taking the kids out there so Chuck and Lilly came over to pick up the kids and I to take us to the hospital. When I walked into the room where he was and I saw the condition he was in I screamed and covered my mouth he looked at me and I ran out the room. Lilly came in the bathroom behind me and asked if I was alright. I turned around and started laughing so hard tears were running down my face. Girl you crazy I thought you were crying and here you are laughing your ass off. What I was so happy to see him all messed up and I can't help but think to myself good for his ass that was no car accident he got his ass whipped. Usually when a man beats on a woman he is a punk ass and cannot handle a man. I know what happened he got caught with someone's woman and her man kicked his ass that's what happened. I started laughing again and all I could say is pay back is a bitch and I did not have to do anything. He came home and sitting on the couch he looks at me and says I know you're happy and you want so bad to kick my ass right now. No I think you did enough of that on your own and I just shook my head. I am not like you James I don't do or dislike people for no reason or do I wish to see a person hurt that did nothing to me that's your job. I know he wanted to talk shit but he could not with both his lips sewed up and holes in his head. Half body brace on looking like a mummy. I thought about pushing him down the stairs and leaving him there no one would have found him and by the time they did it would be too late, but I didn't.

He's all better now he can walk around and go out and all the things that he use to do. With all that going on I found out one thing I was no longer afraid of him all I saw was a weak man and I had nothing to be afraid of. Oh this is it I don't want to hear nothing I am so ready for whatever he got to bring my way. It was almost scary that I felt like that as if I wanted him to try and hit me again I knew if he did I would kill him for sure. He stayed home a lot in the beginning. He started staying out for days and when he would come home I would be so nice and greet him. Honey can I get you something to eat and he would look at me and say hell no you gone try to kill me I am not stupid. What me and the kids ate look I will eat first and then you do it. I will watch and make sure that you eat from the same pot that I do. No problem and I was nice as nice can be and that made him not want to trust me. Later on that night the kids were playing and my son knocked over his drink and then all I heard was screaming and I ran upstairs. He has my son lying on the couch punching him and blood is running out his nose I ran in the kitchen and got the biggest knife I could find. Get away from my son get off him and get the hell out of here now I was ready bring it. He got the hell out of there that night he did not want to see what might happen. He came back after a while and he went downstairs and got in the bed and did not say a word. I just paced the floor upstairs I kept going down stairs to the kid's room acting like I was checking on the kids. I really wanted to see if he was sleeping and when he did I took that same knife and went and sat on the side of the bed looking at him. A part of me say kill him just take the knife and cut his throat. Don't do it he is not worth you going to jail over and what about the kids. He turned around and saw me sitting there he sat up so fast and asked me what am I doing sitting there like that. I told him I just was watching you sleep he said please I am sorry and I just looked at him and told him to go back to sleep. I got up and went upstairs he never saw the knife in my hand.

He notices now that I have a don't give a shit attitude and that I was not taking any more of his shit. One night we had an event for the kids in the community center and he came there drunk looking for me. Asking me where is my son and he walked over to me and swung at me and ripped my earing out my ear and it stared bleeding. I never saw a person fly across a room from a hit except me that is but when I say he flew he flew. See when he attacked me of course security was no joke and like I said we worked close with them. He ran over and grabbed him and literally knocked him across the room and he hit the wall and then hit the floor. The guard put his knee in his chest and took out his gun and looked at me and said what you want me to do? Please don't hurt him and he got up and while everyone was helping me he snatched my son and ran in the apartment. I went with security to the apartment and he said he was not giving him back he wanted him to stay with him. I went back the community center and when I came back to the apartment he was gone. I cried so much I knew he would not hurt him his only son so I thought at the time. He is probably at his mother's house so I could not go there and get him she hated me with a passion probably had his girlfriend taking care of him. One year passed and I did not see my son and finally I guess him and his girlfriend got tired of taking care of him and wanted to give him back. He called me and told me to meet him over Chuck's house and I did. Hi baby and I cried when I saw him and I told him to come to mommy and he said mommy is dead and he would not come to me for nothing in the world. I said mommy is not dead this is mommy and he would not come to me. I got him back and the kids and I went back to Coney Island and I packed my stuff and theirs and called storage and put everything there and we moved out of there. I had called Lorraine and we went over there and I heard he came looking for me and I am sure it was not to say hello but I would have been ready for his ass.

A lot happened after that I was a total bitch in capital letters BITCH and no one could tell me anything especially a man he caught hell. I had so much hate inside me that when I got angry I would black out and not remember what I did and that was scary. One incident the man I was living with got me angry and the next thing I remember is five cops got me on the floor to handcuff me took me to a psychiatric hospital and let me go and he even came and picked me up. When I saw his face I asked what happened to you and he said this is what you did and I knew I had to leave him before I killed him because he was one that nagged and he would have made me crazy. That is how it was anger all bottled up inside me and I had no way of letting it out except to hurt something especially a man. My anger was terrible and after seven years of being beaten I pretty much was a ticking time bomb.

Cocaine that white powder the stuff that makes you think that you got it all together when you really don't the keyword here is THINK. When I started I was not on it like that I had met this guy and he was so cool that I would do it with him once and a while. That's what happens start out with a little and end up with a lot. Even when it got out of control I still thought that I had it under control. But watch how that white powder began to white out my life.

CHAPTER

5

Update # 2

obert was the only one that came to see me in the hospital no even my children came to see me not that I could blame them they hated the way I lived. So what is happening at the apartment I asked Robert? Your apartment is not a crack house there is a line outside to get into your apartment. They pay for a certain amount of time to stay and I believe they get paid with money or drugs whatever the person has to give. What you got keys go over there and tell those mother fuckers to get the hell out my house that I am coming home and I don't want to see anyone there. To tell you the truth I did not even want to come home there are so many things going through my mind I don't know what to do. I wish I had the strength to stop the drugs and lock my door for good and never see any of them again and get my life together. But you see my mother moved to North Carolina and I had no place to go but that didn't matter because when you're on drugs you don't care about anything or anyone.

Robert had cleaned up the house moped the floors and bought some food to put in the house for me. Oh by the way Robert lived in the same building as I did on the other side he took care of his sister in law after his wife died. He rented out his apartment in Harlem and stayed in Brooklyn with her. Whenever I needed something including crack because he knew I was smoking he would sit right there with me. He even knew all the people that came they tried to play me the woman but that was not going to happen. I think he liked the fact that I got high but that was the only reason I was dealing with him I mean really. But I will tell you about that later.

What do you do when day after day you sit there getting high not leaving your house unless you had to go to court or welfare? I mean really how high can you get day after day nonstop I mean after that first high no matter how much you try it's not going to feel that way again never. That's how people fool themselves into thinking they are getting high but in fact they are not.

Staples in my arm was supposed to come out a long time ago and they have not and a cast from toe to hip it's not off yet almost a year. Go ahead you can say it what is wrong with that bitch she got to be stupid she was smoking some shit that nobody else had. Yes and your right I was all fucked up.

CHAPTER

6

Can I get real for a minute?

News always talking about the woman having children and not taking care of them or killing them or someone else they know does it.

Going from here to there with my kids was not a way for them to live and I decided to take them to my sister's house and ask her to please take care of them for me until I was able to take care of them. Until I get myself together is what I told her and she took them. Now you remember that I told you my sister and I did not get along never got along but this is one time I thank God for her. I was not there when they graduated elementary school or junior high school I missed all those precious moments. I kept telling myself I love my children no matter what anyone says. But I didn't have my children so how much do I really love them.

As I write these words down this has to be one of the hardest things I had to do in a very long time. To go back into my life the worst part of it and relive every single detail the good and the bad. Tears is the best way I can describe it is that as I write I know I should have stopped the drugs in order to raise my children. But let's be real about one thing it is so easy for people to past judge me and say a lot of bad things about and I will not be made I get it. But I just want to say unless you been there don't walk in my shoes if they don't fit. If there was a magic word I could have used or said believe me I would have if it could get me where I needed to be. But later I will find out that there was a magic word I could have used, would you like to know what it is?

JESUS – there is something in the name......

I would like to take a minute and talk about my loses while I was a drug addict. My dad I lost him in 1980. While I was a preschool teacher for seven years and yes that is right I was a teacher and a good one at that. My niece and nephew went there along with my kids as well oh yes I still had them then. My sister and I still did not get along but we went together to my parents' house. I screamed when I saw my dad he had to weigh maybe 80lbs and he had just a layer of skin on his body. He could not speak all he was doing is looking up to heaven and moving his mouth really fast. I believe he was talking to God making is peach sought of speaking. He went to the hospital and my sister and I said we would be there tomorrow to see how he was doing. The next day one of my students came to me out of the blue and asked me if I had a father and I said yes what a strange question. Later I would find out that my dad died at the same time he came and asked me that question how weird is that. We went after work but it was too late he had already died. I know we did not get along but I missed him and I wanted to get the chance to tell him I loved him no matter what we felt about one another I loved him and I wanted him to know that. But somehow I feel that he knows I pray that he did. Time to get ready for the wake and the funeral which I thought I was not going to be able to deal with. It could be because of the relationship we had wish I had spent more time with him. I love you daddy is what I told him and then I kissed him and told him he better not wipe off my lipstick want to see it there. Handsome they made him look like he did so many years before healthy bad suit on and always tipped his hat.

Lorraine called me and told me to be strong and she was there for me if I need her she would be there. My best friend was on dialysis and she had been on there since I met her but she was strong and a very good friend. A week after my father died my sister came to my house and she said I got bad news. I looked at her and told her I cannot take any more bad news please I don't want to hear it. Is it mommy please is she ok? Mommy is fine but Lorraine died yesterday. I believe my heart stopped beating for a second I could not talk at all my heart was broken I felt like I was going to die. Oh God no please why is this happening she was fine I spoke to here last week, just the other day how could this be. Her son oh no her son what is he doing who has him where is her I have to get him he should not be there alone right now. Slow down my sister said. I went out and called her mother and she let me talk to her son and he said mommy can you come and get me? I am coming I will be there tomorrow promise and he wanted the kids so to see them and I was heartbroken. I went to the wake for some reason I could not go up to the casket to say goodbye I had to do it from the back and when her son saw me he said you don't want to go and see mommy? I can't I love her and I am so hurt that I cannot go up there I loved her so much and I was hugging him and crying at the same time. When can I come to your house and I spoke to his grandmother and she said I can come and get him whenever I wanted. I will be there tomorrow to get him and take him for the week if that was ok. He turned to her and begged her and she said yes and we had a great time. I pray that I can find him again have not seen him since I pray he is ok.

My favorite Uncle ever died three months after his brother my father died. Everyone said he was heartbroken when he lost his brother that he did not want to live without him. The thing with that is they looked just a like they were twins and they were buried in the same suit and coffin and funeral pallor. Too much I tell you too much to take please Lord don't let anyone else die please. I would say about 93 I lost Chucks wife Lilly my best friend in the world. We partied our ass off had so much fun together love you. Robert died in 86 my daughters father died in 86 and so did James.

And look I am still here!!!

Chapter

7

What's its going to be?

One summer day in well let me say around 84 I think. Now you see what I mean about that white powder whites out stuff. I am at Lilly's house and I turn around and I see my children and they said before I can ask our Aunt said that we cannot stay there to go and find you and let you decide what to do with us. I could not believe that she did that not knowing if I was here or not how could she do that. But first they told me they went to their grandmother's house and she said we could not stay there either, so we spent the night and she sent us back to our Aunts house. I bet there were saying to themselves is she going to be able to take care of us or is she going to take us someplace else and leave us. They remember coming to see me when I was in the mental institution. Yes you heard right mental institution I was there twice and I had to get the hell out of there. Sad to say I was very suicidal thought I would be better off dead who would miss me. My children probably hated me and well the rest of my family could not care less so why am I here. I signed myself in and they put me on medication was terrible and I was there for a minute I would go in front of the doctor and talk with him so he can see what progress I made. Although I signed myself in the board will decide what to do if I stayed or left. Thank God I was able to come home I did feel much better but the medication they sent me home with I had to get rid of it and never took them again. I remember when I came out I looked back and thought about the time I was a worker in that ward today I leave as a patient. Life is funny how things happen a crystal ball is what I needed if only

There is no room at Lilly's house or I would have been able to stay there but I could not and she felt bad about me having to leave. I asked myself are you ready for this it has been a while since you had the role of a mother? As I stood there I looked at them and I thought how much they have grown these are my kids wow. They looked at me wondering what is she going to do I know they were afraid I would not want them. Those were my babies so what's its going to be? Mommy where are we going are we going to stay with you. I said well your Aunt don't want you and your grandmother don't want you. We are going to PA because we are all three homeless and don't worry we will be ok. Ok mommy and those words sounded so good to hear yes its time you be a mother to your children. I was pissed for my sister doing that and at my mother too so I said they will never have to worry about my children ever again. We went to PA and they said that we would have to wait for placement but it did not take long before we were headed in a van to Manhattan going to Catherine Street shelter. Now I have been in a shelter before but not my children and this is much different from the one that I was in which was a woman's shelter. In the beginning we were a little uncomfortable not a little but a lot. We were sleeping in a big room on cots and one locker with adults and children. Well this is home and we have to make the best of it for now at least were all together. When I thought about it that was all that mattered and finally I was with my children and it felt good I was there to protect them. Catherine St shelter was not bad after all after being there for a while they started doing work on the last two floors and they said the only families that will be able to move up there are those that gave them no problems. There would be two families per room and there you can have your own TV and bring food was different same rules but different. Of course we were chosen to move there and the kids were so happy they had made their little friends and was in school. Now I got food stamps and cash so I made sure they had what they needed. I waited before I called my mother because I know by now my sister had told her what she did and my mother told her the same thing. So I called her and I told her I don't think it was fair what her and my sister did to the kids and she would not have to worry about seeing them again because I was not bring them to see her and not letting them come to see her. I have my children and I am their mother so don't worry they are fine. I am glad to hear that Rosalind after all they are your children and if you did not want them that is your decision to put them in foster care. Ok mommy I have to go I will talk to you soon. Rosalind don't hang up the phone please I don't want to end this conversation like this don't be mad if you need me you know how to get me. But we don't need anything from you mommy we are fine they are in school and they have new clothes and we are fine and I hung up the phone.

Things are going ok new place new faces new people to meet. I would say friends but remember a shelter is not a place that you want to meet friends. This is temporary and friends don't last long because most of them are not real. Let me explain to those of you who might read this book. When you go into a shelter with children it's called a family shelter. After being there for a certain amount of time you go to what is called a tier two shelter. This is where you get your own apartment still in a shelter but you have your own apartment as if you was not in a shelter. The good thing about that is you don't have to be in at 10pm no curfew. Still have rules and if you don't do right they can put you out. Now crack was around heavier and I was doing it but not as much as I would when I move from there. Before moving to a tier two I had a lump in my breast and I needed to have a biopsy so I had to leave me kids and go have it and come home a couple of hours after that. When I got back they told me they had a tier two for us to move to and in all my pain I packed all our stuff and we got in the van and went to the Bronx. I left the bags in the van because if I did not like it we was going right back to Catherine Street, what the hell is this. It was dark and horrible one room with three cots and a little fridge and the bathroom was in the hallway. Let's go kids and back we went to the shelter. They let me go back to my room and the next day they called me and said they had an opening at Henry Street

Settlement. Now that was one of the best tier two shelters in NY and I was not going to pass that up. This is great one bedroom with two beds in there and in the living room a day bed with a bed underneath that one. Dining room set and came with brand new dishes, silverware and pots this was beautiful. When thanksgiving came around I had my first dinner there I cooked for the first time in a long time. And it was good my family came over my sister and my mother and brother. My niece even came and stayed with us for a while. I found a place to buy cocaine and it was good better then Brooklyn look at me comparing cocaine like it was clothes or food. To avoid buying crack I would cook up my own and of course I got high a lot by myself. Since I did get high by myself a lot one time I snorted so much cocaine my heart started beating so fast as though it was going to stop I would snort just a little boy and that would bring me down slow my heartbeat. I could have died from all that cocaine but of course Jesus was there and kept me and I did not even say thank you.

I always tried to keep myself looking good so that I don't look like a crack head although you cannot cover that up. I was always small but now I am really small. I always said if they make cocaine legal doctors could subscribe it to lose weight. I have never seen a crack head or cocaine user that weighed 200lbs.

Now everything might be going ok but things were slowing falling apart. I was getting high too often and too much. My son started getting in trouble I started messing up bad. But I did not take no shit from no one and they knew that I would put them in their place and had no problem beating your ass neither. How much can you be in control and you're getting high and your kids know what you're doing. How much are they going to respect you and when you want to so call sit down and talk with them and ask for forgiveness they don't want to hear you? You can beat them and have them in check but your word is garbage. Say what you mean but don't mean what you say yes if that works for you. My son said to me ma you didn't think about us when you was cashing in food stamps for us to eat you didn't think about us and you want us to forgive you. That I will always remember until this day and he made me cry that day I cried for a long time. That would not be the last time that I disappointed my children. People this is what drugs do I don't care what kind you on don't fool yourself that's for all that's to all those under cover get high.

Erving was the best thing that happened to me I met him when I was in the shelter no he did not live there he was so nice and he cared about my children. He would call me and tell them to come to his job and get money to buy sneakers or whatever they needed. He was wonderful he would take us out together and eat and to the movies. He lived with his mother in the projects in Brooklyn my mother loved him. He worked for NYC Housing and complaints and when they called me to the office and said I was denied by housing for an apartment. I called him screaming and crying and he told me to stop crying and he gave me the address to the mayor's office and he told me what to write and I did it. About a week later I got a letter in the mail and it said the decision was over turned and I could get an apartment from housing. That was really good news now I can get my son away from here. They called me in the office too and told me the good news and I told them I got the same letter. I could not wait to go and look at some apartments I was happy. I got up the following week to go and meet with the person from housing to see some apartments. The first one I did not like but the second one I went to see is the one I took two bedrooms. Remember that crystal ball I was talking about I wish I had one during this time. If I would have had one I would have known that this would be the place where I would almost die.

I got back to the shelter and started packing and told the kids that we were leaving going back to Brooklyn and they were happy about that. We are going to have our own apartment again. Yes again this will be the third apartment I had with my kids the first two was not too bad but this one will turn out to be the worst one of all. Try and remember before the kids I was a great mother was just in a horrible relationship. When will I get it right.........

We moved and Erving bought the kids bunk beds for their bedroom and my mother bought me my dining room set. I was a drug addict so of course I had my rent go directly to housing this way we will have a roof over our head and I will never again let my children not have food to eat I learned that lesson. I was no stranger to the area I used to live not far from there my running buddies still lived there my best friend was like a sister to me and my kids called her auntie. My mother and brother still lived in Canarsie and that was a short bus trip to get there. My sister lived like 20 minute walk so we were close to everyone. My children had friends around there that they knew from school so we were fine. Only the people were strange and the surroundings is where the real terror lied. No one knew me so when I would see my kids outside people would say that's your mom. Not bragging back in that time they looked more like my brother and sister. Ok maybe I am over exaggerating but not too much.

Things were looking good now but soon they will get very ugly real fast.

CHAPTER

8

Road to ruins

As I write the words to this book I have to stop. Reliving this part of my life is not easy this is so unreal to know that this really happened. All of it I am not even telling because if I did this would be one of the biggest books ever written I mean except for the Bible. This is going to sound crazy but I feel better after writing these words it's as if they leave me and remain trapped in these pages. Someone will read this and they will say there is no way and someone is going through the same thing right now. Read this book, I am telling you no matter what it is you're going through you are going to be just fine. You will not experience half of the things that I went through but I am a living witness that you can do this. Someone is reading this rather you're on the train or at work at home or in a shelter. Remember one thing that all things are possible no matter what you're going through. If I can come through I know you can too I know right now you feel that all hope is gone. There was a light that was always there but I could not see it. Don't think this book will end with a fairy tale ending because it does not. The ending of this story is a reality ending something you can identify with. Hold on tight because as you finish reading this book you will see that as bad as things got for me, I'll tell you what just keep reading and you will see. Please don't give up whatever you do don't give up hold on help is on the way. Change is good only if you want it and don't let anybody tell you different.

I called this chapter ruins because as you can see I was headed in the right direction but then again I could not have been headed in the right direction and still an addict. I went from coke head to full blown crack addict. Crack is no joke and I want to express that to the person reading this book if you smoke crack you don't have shit under control. Don't lie to yourself and think that I do it once in a while I don't give a dam about how many times you do it you still do it. Little do you know you lost that control the day you snorted a line or the day you picked up that pipe and put the rock in side and it started sizzling and you pulled. Your control went right out the window with all your other values you held so dear. You found your best friend and just like your best friend everything went up in smoke. How did you feel when you saw that thick white smoke coming down that glass pipe and you slowly exhale and...... yeah but I bet you didn't know you will never get that same high again I don't care how good that shit is you buy. Never ever again will you feel back so go head keep buying those dimes it aint gone happen. Say good bye because that person you was before you took that pull is gone bye bye. It's sad to know that so many people die not knowing how their life could have been without the cloud following them. Grace

Ok so were are settled in our new place and I don't know too much of anything around there not yet that is. Ok I got Robin now that's my girl she was like my sister for real. We go way back to the time when I was a preschool teacher he daughter was my student that is how we met. She would go home and talk about me to her parents and on open school is when I met her and after that it was on we were good. Our children were very close and to reconnect with everyone was good we had a great time when we got together. After I went into the shelter I did not see Lilly but now I see her all the time we party she would come over and it was like ole times only now I had my own place. There was a club two blocks from my house and we use to go there all the time I went every Friday. Of course I had to find out where the cocaine was and it did not take long three blocks I was good. Funny how you don't know anyone and when someone sees you going to a certain place you find people want to know who you are. I had my own apartment to get high in I did not have to go to someplace else to get high. My children already knew what was going on but I gave them respect just the same. If you ever got high you know that if someone came to your house to smoke they had to give to the house and that was me of course. Out of a 24 hour day there would be maybe 2 hours that I did not have people in my house. I would not have just one or two persons in my house I am talking about 15-20 there and I know you're wondering why. See I would not just get high I was the type that played music and played cards not just sit and get high. So when you came to my house you had something to do fun stuff no fighting no arguing. I must say though this crack is so strong that I saw it make people react a certain way that made me laugh. Some people could not take noise when they smoked then you came to the wrong place. I am not the one thinking you can come and tell me to be quiet in my own house hell to the no. Others would start picking at their skin I mean some really messed up stuff but you're in control, whatever!

But with all those so called friends, sorry smoking partners I meant to say laughing and bullshitting with me was nothing. I tell you this much that day I got that knock on my door not one person was in my house not one. Any other time I had a house full of people that day not one person showed up like they were warned not to come or they will have to get a beat down. Yeah where was you so called crack heads then?

Things were out of control for the short four years that I lived there so many things happened that felt like I was on a roller coaster. My son left the house he was tired of me stealing from him so he no longer wanted to live there. My daughter was expecting and she did not want bring the baby home there and I don't blame her, she got her own apartment. Now I am all alone without the children that I moved there with and ask me did I care hell no of course I did not. I had my pipe that was all I needed everything else did not matter. That is what I meant when I said that my whole life went up with that white cloud. Yes that's right I was that crack head who thinks she got it all together . You know it's bad when your own mother comes to your house and you don't want to put the pipe down long enough to see her. Now on top of your kids leaving your mother has now moved to North Carolina. All is lost gone up in smoke and every time I would put that lighter to that pipe who was now my best and only friend. With every pull and with every white cloud that came out that pipe that was my life coming out of my body. You still don't get it do you if I liked it Satan loved it. I mentioned earlier that I would find out what Rev. Washington was trying to save me from. But Satan had me right where he wanted me under his control and power and I did not have the power to get out of his grip. I needed help but I did not know how to ask for it eventually I will but not right now it's like I did not want to get out of this death trap. It will still be a while before I would say those words that I needed to say so desperately. My mother often wrote me letters after she moved in early 1992. But later that year in October she would pray harder for me than she ever did before. Oh she has been praying for me long before now but her prayers went unanswered for a very long time. God was listening and He heard her but it's not her cry's He wanted to hear they were mine. God waited for me after all He was there all the time. I have proof of that I am telling the story right.

CHAPTER

9

Finally we're up to date

Now its 1993 and here I am still sitting here in this house with this cast still on my leg and sometimes I feel likes something is crawling inside. I was too afraid at that point to go to the hospital thinking I would lose my leg. My mother came up that Christmas and she wanted me to come over my sister's house to see her. Of course I went and all I kept hearing is why the cast was still on my leg but of course I had a reason a crack head usually does. I could not wait to get out of there I need a hit and a cigarette. My mother went back and I think she wrote me every week telling me how much she loved me and how she was praying for me and all the motherly things that a mom tells her daughter. She said I need to stop what I was doing it was only causing more pain for me. Of course I cried when I was reading her letters to know that is what she was doing as well. Then I would take a hit and that white cloud would just make all that go away.

The shape that I was in with the cast on things started happening that would not have happened before the cast was on. But although I was a crack head I still had a kind heart and if anyone would come to me and needed a place to sleep I would provide them with that. People took my kindness for a sign of weakness so I got tired of that real fast and did not want to be bothered with them anymore.

Robert came over one day and he was upset about his apartment in Harlem where he let some people stay there I don't know what happened but he was pissed. Put them out if it got you that upset. What he said as he turned around looking at me and I said that's right put out because I want to move there. He started laughing at me I mean he was laughing hard too and said you know good and well you aint leaving here. You get there and after a week you will tell me you want to come back because you know I cannot stay there with you. I am ready to leave here so please put them out I am ready to go. Your serious he looked at me and saw my face and I said yes I am very serious. What about your furniture what are you going to do with that? Leave it leave all of it all I want is my clothes that I have a little things that's all I want. Ok I will go over there in the morning and I said no call them right now because I want to be in there this week. I can honestly say that he loved me no matter what he did and then I would think that is it because of the drugs. See when I was smoking he was able to do things to that I liked and real freaky shit but I was high I did not care.

Nobody knows I am leaving and that is the way I want to keep it until the day I was leaving and everybody laughed at me then I told them I was playing but I was not. I wanted to disappear on them like everyone disappeared on me that day. I left that night not the next day with a couple of bags with my clothes and I said goodbye to the memories from HELL. I will go to Harlem where I would start new memories. So off I went moving again to a new place and new people. Now don't think I went there to get off the drugs I just wanted to get high now in peace without the drama. I told him he knew he had to bring me some stuff after all he knew everyone there he lived there long enough. He knew who was doing what and where yeh nothing changed for me same high just a different borough. So I was fine in Harlem just fine I had what I needed and I was good. Robert would come over every day because his sister in law had someone to stay with her during the day. He would come and bring me what I needed not just drugs but food whatever I needed. I need to go to Harlem hospital to see about getting this cast off. You will never guess who went with me to the hospital yeah my sister came with me. She said that she did not want to come in the room with me when they took it off and the people there did not believe me when I told them how long I had it on. When they took it off I could not believe the way it looked the doctor told me that he was surprised that it looked that good. Good doc if that is good then I would hate to see what bad would look like. He said at least you still have it. Right about that and it looked like a tree and skinny like a branch. He said that the dead skin will fall off eventually and I would need physical therapy for a long time to even be able to put pressure on that leg. I had to keep a special covering on the leg and soak it so the dead skin could come off. I was in therapy three days a week and it was painful. Now because of my stupid and dumb actions that the crack effect had on me to cause me to keep a cast on my leg all that time was crazy. And for the rest of my life I will suffer as a result of my drug use. Why you ask well I don't have hip movement on my right hip and my leg does not bend back. I cannot stand straight because of it so I put all my weight on my left leg. So I walk with a limp its noticeable and sometimes I see the looks I get. I cannot lift my right foot because I had the cast on from my toes to my hip the cast stared falling down crushing my ankle. This is what I call the after effects of crack cocaine for me it caused a lot more trouble than I thought it would. So you see I have a constant reminder of my life of being a drug addict the pain is the only thing I have to remind me of that terrible life. But I am alive so the pain is more like a victory pain now. I told Robert to find my daughter and let her know where I am and give her the phone number oh yeah that's right I had a phone it might sound stupid but I was excited. I know she will tell my son where I was and give him the number too. My daughter now has two children a girl and a boy and my son has a daughter. I did not see his daughter or his girlfriend but I was about to meet them for the first time. My son probably said don't bring my daughter over there to see her but my daughter I don't care what I was or what I was doing she wanted to see her mother.

Time was passing and Robert decided that he did not want to leave me alone anymore in Harlem he wanted to move there. What about your sister in law you cannot leave her there by herself at night. He did not leave her he would come and get a couple of feels as long as I was getting high I did not care but if I was sober hell no I hated for him to touch me. The people he would send to get my stuff I met so when he was not there I would just call them out the window and he did not like that he was jealous. One day I was looking out the window just looking we lived on the 2nd floor window in the front I loved looking out the window the people you see amazing. But one day I was looking the window and I saw a guy come up the stairs out the next building. All I can say is that he was so fine I mean he had a body and looks to go with that body. I could not look away I wanted to but I could not I put a big smile on my face as if I was 16 years old. He smiled back and said how you doing my heart stopped beating and fine was my reply. People thought Robert was my father and not my man his whole head of hair was white and he walked with a cane. If we was outside he would let everyone know that I was his wife. If I was in the window and he was outside I was his wife no matter who he was talking to. What an old man like you doing with this young lady and he would say ask her I am glad no one asked me that question. I loved Robert in my own way he was a very good man and he was taking care of me what more can I ask for. Oh boy here comes that fine sexy man again as he walked toward me and Robert standing outside talking to a lady that lived in the next building. Hi ma he said to the lady that we was talking to and he said hello to us to and I said hello with a smile on my face. Robert walked away to speak to someone and I said to her is that your son? Yeah he is but your man catch you speaking to him he gone kill you I can tell he jealous. I thought to myself he is worth it for sure I won't mind getting in trouble for him.

My sister called me and said that her and my niece were going to North Carolina to see my mother and asked me if I wanted to go. I did not really want to go but I told her I will go to see my mother I have not seen her in a long time.

CHAPTER

10

Mommy & Grand's

It's a different world there in the south nice and quiet and a very beautiful there I mean everything about it was great. My mother sat me down in the back yard and told me that she had a message from the Lord that she had to tell me. Oh boy another sermon do she think I really want to hear this right now. I heard it anyway and she said I better get myself together because the next time God might not show me mercy the next time. Yes mommy I know I changed and knowing the whole time I was talking to her I was thinking about my friend back home the pipe and I know that God knew it too can't hide anything from Him. Love you mommy talk to you when I get home.

Robert came down to help me with the bags and said his good byes to my family. I was glad we lived on the second floor after that long ride my legs were killing me. Roberts's sister in law passed away and they had her body right across the street from where we lived. There was so many funeral homes there like sometime two on each block.

My daughter started coming over and bringing my grandchildren with her to see me. I was on PA and getting a lot of food stamps. Even my other granddaughter came to see me my son's daughter and I felt somewhat human again. My son was away at the time and when his girlfriend would bring my granddaughter over he would call and I would be able to speak to him. Mind you I have not seen or spoken do my son way before the accident in Brooklyn. Wow I am back in touch with my children and I even have to pleasure of seeing my grands cannot ask for anything more than that. But my life was far from good that is why I said I felt somewhat human again. In a minute all that would change.

CHAPTER

11

Something about That Name

Smoking, smoking, smoking but now I am not as skinny as I was before I put on a little weight. I was going to therapy three times a week so I could not go there high so I had to slow down a little. It was a weekend Friday and I started smoking and its now Saturday and I am still smoking. Robert got tired of staying up and he figured he'd better go to sleep while I still had a lot left before I ask him to go outside and get me some more crack. So there I sat at the table with all my pipes and crack and for some reason I began to cry. I mean I was crying like someone whipped my ass that kind of crying. I cannot explain it but at that moment I looked up to Heaven and I called on Him and I said Jesus please help me. I don't want to do this anymore I am tired and I need your help. Please help me Jesus please I beg you I will do whatever you say. Please save me please I don't want to live like this anymore I must have cried for about 20 minutes. When I stopped a peace came over me that I cannot explain I have never felt this before in my life. I just sat there looking up and I called Robert and he got up I asked him to get me a bag and I threw everything away. Why you doing that so you can have me get another pipe and crack in a couple of days. No I am not going to ask you for anything.

Well now this is something that even I can't believe, Jesus was just sitting there on the right hand of God the Father waiting for me to call His name. Just to think that is all I had to do is call His name all this time that is all I had to do. Now I know what the song Something About The Name Jesus there is power and healing in the name. Days turned into weeks and weeks into months and I thought to myself what crack did I ever smoke that I mean that is what Jesus did for me. Robert could not believe it all I did was read my Bible all day and pray. Oh boy you talk about getting back all the things that the enemy had stolen Jesus gave it all back.

I called my mother and started telling her how good God was he screamed and started crying she could not believe she was talking to her daughter. She said she got her daughter back and all cleaned up. Your voice sounds different you don't even sound like the same person. I am not the same person mommy I am a child of God and I don't do the same thing like I used to nothing I do is the same.

Robert was not happy about that I would not let him touch me I had to sit him down and talk with him and tell him it was the drugs that is why I would let him touch me. I told him I cared for him but not enough to continue like that but I will try my best to love him. Although I was only fooling myself and lying to him knowing I would never want him to touch me again. Now you may say that is cold the man took you in his house and took care of you when no one else would. But understand this I think he is upset because he no longer had control over me I did not need him anymore to supply me with drugs that is what he missed. He liked me better when I was getting high and that is the truth.

Hey how are you doing long time no see this is a guy that use to live with me in Brooklyn and Robert knew him? He saw him in Brooklyn and told me that he did not get high anymore and I said well good for him. Why is it so hard for people to believe when a person stops getting high it's like unbelievable. I said yeah Robert told me and I don't either been months now since I stopped. He looked at Robert and he said that's right she just stopped all she do now is read the Bible and listen to gospel songs. He was my runner that is someone that goes out and buys drugs for you and of course he go drugs in return. But sometimes you send him and he would take a long time and when he did come back he said he got busted but you know that was a lie he smoked your shit and told that lie. There was a girl that he was messing with and he told her about me that is after he found out that I was not getting high anymore. I can tell that he was surprised and no one has seen me since I left in the middle of the night.

Robert had a good friend that lived in the next building and he loved Robert like a father. He use to come over I loved him a lot he was so real and nothing to joke with. His apartment was very nice I would go over sometimes and visit. He would always come to the house and get some of Roberts food he sure was able to cook I did nothing at all. Bill would come over and we would laugh and act crazy. I asked him one day while I was curling his hair oh yes he would have me curl his hair, what Church did he go to and he said right up the block girl you need to come with me one day. I will come with you next week and he said don't play with me you better be ready service is at 11 sharp. Hello are you almost ready and he said don't worry about me I will call you from the window. The Church was located on W123rd Street and Lenox and I liked it so much that the following Sunday I joined the Church and the Gospel Choir and did my first solo the following Sunday. "We Don't Get In the Spirit" that was the first song I did and I tore it up for the Lord I sang that song. Yes with all the smoking and drinking I have done God gave me a gift a voice. I told you how I use to play my music when I got high I had some people tell me that if I ever stopped smoking I would have a contract that is how good I sounded. So once I started singing for the Lord I knew I was going to be good at that I was singing His praises and I had a good reason to do so. He saved my life!! After that it seemed like every Sunday I was leading a song. I would bring new songs to the choir that I had all the cd's to and they had never heard them so we would tear it up when we sang we sang and there was nothing no one could tell us we knew we was bad. I mean let me not forget that the reason we sounded so good is because we was singing for Jesus. I knew every word to every song on every gospel tape I had. I always had new songs for the choir and they loved that they was hearing songs they never heard before. Now are you ready for this I starting writing gospel songs and I got a recorder and I took the recorder to my Pastor and let him listen to it. He said that it sounded good and I was so happy and proud and thankful for the gift God gave me. I believe the next Sunday I directed the Youth Choir and I must say in rehearsal they were good but when it came time to sing they killed it. I can still remember how I felt when they read from the bulletin and it was time for them to sing and I got up from my seat and I gave them the signal to stand. Everyone said ok go head Rosalind and when they started singing you would think that I had been directing them for years. They killed it they were so good. After they sang everyone was on their feet. Pastor said I thought for sure I was in the recording studio that did not sound live that sounded like a recording. He even mentioned not only can she sing she writes gospel songs too. He said that God was working in the Church and things were changing and looking up. Yes He was working because if you want to see a miracle then just take a look at me, I am proof of God's work. That is another reason I wrote this book for those of you who don't believe as I once did. Just continue reading and you will see that it's never too late I don't care what you have been through there is something about the name JESUS.

Now things are going well for me and with me and my sons girlfriend brought my granddaughter to see me and she called him your mother changed. What do you mean she changed what is different about her. He did not believe her so she told him to call me and speak to me and he will see for his self that I had indeed changed. She came over another time and she came over and he called and I accepted the call and he said hello and I said hi son how are you. Ma is that really you I did not believe her when she said that you changed but you sound so different. I know I cannot wait to see you when you get home do you need anything? If you can send me a couple of dollars that's all I need. What I am going to send you a package with all the things you like and some money. Ok mama thank you and I love you and I love you too son. His girlfriend called me the next day and she wanted to tell me how happy he was that he had his mama back.

I know things were going well and everything was wonderful but what I did not know is that Satan was very upset to hear that I called on the name of Jesus to get away from his grip. What no drugs and going to Church and singing His praises. No way let me see if I can get her back if only for a little while.

The smoke from the pipe had cleared but little did I know that the cloud was getting closer and closer over my head. Pretty soon the white thick cloud of smoke that I had forgot will soon rear its ugly head. Just to remind me of how good it use to feel like the first time.

CHAPTER

12

In the Christian language it's called Backsliding

Hello I answered it was late and I wanted to know who was calling at that time. Hi is this Rosalind and I said yes it is. This is Cheryl a friend of Bobby's he told me about you and I wanted to talk to you to see if you can help me. Yes Hi Cheryl how are you and the baby doing and she went on to tell me that Brian was in jail. I am sorry is he ok I did not know he did not call me. I know but will it be ok if I can come and speak to you please. Of course you can she said that I will be there tomorrow after work. She came over like she said after work and I sat there playing with the baby and she wanted to know if I could keep the baby for her while she went to work or a couple of days. And I told her sure I will do it to help her out and she did say that she was going to pay me so I could use the extra money. The last day of my watching the baby I asked her if they had any openings at her job I will do whatever. She called me the next morning and she told gave me the job address and she told me who to ask for when I got to personnel. She said that she would meet me outside and take me up to personnel. I have not worked in I don't remember how long

I hope the drugs didn't affect my brain cells. But I know that God can open doors that had been closed no matter how long because there is nothing that He cannot do.

When can you start and of course my answer was right away and he said ok than see you Monday morning at 9am. Thank you very much and as I was saying that I was rejoicing inside saying thank you Jesus. Told you there was power in the name Jesus. This is a whole new beginning and I have everything to be thankful for a new life with no drugs. Since that day I called His name I have been blessed over and over again. Everything that I had lost my God gave back to me my family and grand's and siblings and now a new job. I never thought this would happen to me I am forever grateful and thankful for the great work that He has done for me.

Guess what my job is I was mail room supervisor head of the mailroom for both buildings. I met with the supervisor in charge and I was the happiest person in the world. That meant that 8am I had to be at the post office and pick up the mail and I mean stacks of mail bags. Take a cab and get a receipt so I can get paid back from the company. Sort the mail I had my own office where I did that at and deliver to 6 floors and the building across the street. I did in house mail to from the president's office and everything else. That was a lot of work and I had my own stamp machine and put postage and send out the mail. That included Fed Ex, UPS and regular mail.

Do you remember that fly guy I was telling you about his name is Danny. I used to act like a little kid around him and he knew it. He had a girlfriend a young girl and as you may know he was also much younger than I was too. She would follow him wherever her went. On Saturday I was looking out the window and I saw him my old man had went to the store so he looked up and said hi how are you? He stood there and said I am coming up I want to tell you something. He came upstairs and I was standing at the door waiting for him as if I could care what he had to tell me. He walked up to me and I thought I would die she came so close to me and he was shorter than I was but his body oh my goodness what can I say. He looks at me and says I don't think we were properly introduced my name is and I stopped him. Hardly breathing I said I know Danny and I am Rosalind. He came closer and took my hand and gave me a kiss that I thought for a minute I was floating really. I will see you later and just in case you have not noticed every day you get off the bus I am sitting outside. I tell my mother I really like her and she said don't do it that ole man be looking out the window waiting for her to get off that bus or either he is standing outside. One day I told him don't worry you can come to my job and see me we can find a way to see each other.

I think I am in love and I had to tell myself no you're not in love with that boy. I know that I wanted him and I would find a way to get him if it was possible. And that I did he came to the job and we went out to lunch. Sitting at the table acting like little high school kids kissing one another smiling the whole nine. That is the affect he had on me and I like it very much, I could not wait to get off the bus everyday knowing that he was going to be there. As I crossed the street he was undressing me with his eyes and I was doing the same. One day I got off the bus and my ole man was standing outside and I know he saw Danny staring at me it was no way not to notice. I was trying not to look at him and blushing the whole time. The ole man starting acting up after that would start arguments for no reason but I did not care.

My first Choir Anniversary and I invited all my family to come and see what I been up to and come to Church and support me. They all showed up and I was very happy and my son was home that made me feel good. The ole man is still acting up real bad and it was so bad that I had met an older man on the job that I was dealing with before Danny. Why is she doing this to him you're asking why is she treating him like that he has been really good to her. Really listen I told you the only reason he was there from jump street was to keep me supplied up with drugs and I would not leave him as long as he gave me what I wanted. I was using him and he was using me that is the only thing we had in common. But when the drugs stopped we stopped simple as that. He knew he had lost me and there was nothing that he could do about it. He could no longer satisfy me sexually because no drugs no love period. So now you say why I didn't just move if that was the case. I was going to leave but he begged me not to and he went as far as telling me he wanted to marry me and he was going to buy me a nice engagement ring and marry me that's all he wanted to do. I knew that he would need someone to take care of him eventually he was much older than I was and I did not hate him I just never loved him.

The job is going well and Danny and I are seeing more and more of each other at work mostly. I noticed when I would meet Danny for lunch I would have a drink or two and that was something that I had stopped when the drugs stopped. I would tell myself as long as I am not doing drugs than I am ok. But it was not because I started drinking more and more. God had given me everything that I ever wanted so why am I acting as though this is ok when I know it's not. I had no answer I was not reading the Bible anymore and I began to forget all about the hell that I was living in and where God had brought me from. I thought everything was ok and I did not need Him anymore I had what I needed. I was not calling on His name like I was when I was first touched by the precious saving Grace. One Friday Danny met me after work and we went down the block to a bar. We was having a great time until he told me he had to leave and I started to get angry and drank more and told him to leave so he kissed me and left. Boy did I get drunk that night. My ole man was looking out the window when I got off the bus and I saw one of the guys that use to go and buy my drugs for me and I told him to come in the hallway. I gave him money and told him to buy me a new stem and some good crack and hurry up. You drunk and so fuckin what, just go and do what I asked. What the hell is wrong with you and I said hi honey I'm home and he started laughing. He came to help me upstairs I had to go to the bathroom so bad but didn't make it. What have you been drinking and I said everything. Joe is going to call you from the window I sent him to the store. What the hell you doing you going to start doing that again as if he wasn't happy if I did. Don't worry just this one time and that's it no more don't worry I am not going back I just want something right now. I was thinking about Danny how was I letting a man cause me to smoke crack stupid ass hole that what I was saying to myself in my mind. Get the cards out the closet and go get me one beer no three beers and hurry up. Yes honey he said with a big smile on his face. He was very happy have not seen him that happy in a very long time.

I lied that was not the only time I was acting like a maniac for real I was even scaring my own self. I started messing up on the job staying out a lot just not wanting to go outside or do anything. There is something happening this time it was different not like the last time I got high. I was acting different it was as though some kind of unseen power that was dead set on destroying me. I called the President of my Choir and I was telling her what was going on with me and she told me to come to Church so we can pray together. I did but it did not help I was too ashamed to ask God for help I knew He was mad at me and probably would not want to help me again. He saved my life and gave me everything back and this is what I do with it. I really messed up now. Now I really messed up I started smoking on Friday and its now 6am Monday morning and I am still smoking. I left to go to work at 12pm and went to talk to my supervisor and made up lies and told her I had an emergency and she gave me advances on my pay and extra. I left and went home and what did I do? Come on it don't take now rocket scientist to figure that one out.

I had started getting sick I could not work has not been there for two weeks and one day I just called my supervisor and told her I needed to talk to her. I was so ashamed to talk to her but I had to do something.

My supervisor was a black woman and she lived in Bedford Sty and she did not play at all she was street smart as well. Let's go to the conference room and talk. We sat down and she sat right across from me and she said so tell me Rosalind what's going on. I already know but I need you to tell me and I just started crying breaking down. I lied to you about everything and I am using drugs. What it must be cocaine some kind of form the mood swings you have and all the other signs. I watch you walk around some days you're so cheerful they can't want for you to come on the floor. But then there are other days that you don't say a word hardly know you came on the floor everyone noticed. Everybody likes you in here they love you when I hear laughing I know you're on the floor. You need to get help your too good to let that take over there is so much more to live for. I cannot say that the job will be here waiting for you because it will not be. But I pray that you get the help that you need and if you need to talk just call me and I said thank you and I got up to leave. Wait she handed me a check and she told me to call her next week and she would give me 2weeks vacation pay. Thank you so much and I walked out the door never to return again.

I know you think this is it she is going to end this book with her in rehab and never getting her life together. Well you're wrong about me although the previous chapters looked really dim and my Iife well did not have much light in it. But like I said earlier this is not a fairy tale ending but for me it's the best ever!

Well that was that the end of another chapter in my well life.....

CHAPTER

13

The Road Is Long

Ever heard those lyrics "the road is long with many a winding turns that leads to who knows where who knows when" that is so true. You know if I did not know any better you would think that someone cast some kind of spell on me I don't believe in that kind of stuff things were bad enough without letting something or someone mess with my mind. This is some tiring shit really I mean this is like a 9-5 kind of thing going on here. The work that I put into messing up my life I got a degree in that. Listen I always said that I have and educational degree and a street degree and they both are good to have in away. I had common sense the elevator did not always go to the top floor but it moved.

I can't disappoint my children again they were so happy to have their mother back and my family was happy too. I spent time with my grandchildren I even potty trained my 3 grandchildren. I don't know how they are going to feel about this and I don't know how they are going to react. The one thing that I do know is that I have to get out of this apartment and away from this man. If I stay I am sure that my life will be over and that God will never allow me to get back what I threw away.

I called my sons wife and asked her if she was going to be home and she automatically asked me what was wrong. I need to talk to you and my son I have a problem and I need to get away from Harlem and you know who. Come over now and put some clothes in a bag and come over here right now. Thank you and I will call you when I am leaving or getting off the train over there. You're not going to change your mind are you don't call me back and say that you're not coming or you will be here tomorrow or next week. I am not going to do that I will be there I promise. I was outside I could not call from in the house he was listening to everything I said and now I have to go and get some clothes and deal with him. Nothing was going to change my mind I am going and that was it no matter what he said I am leaving today. I felt as if my life was going to end if I stayed one more day. I told him everything without an interruptions I asked that he please hear me. I told him everything about my job that I told my boss I was an addict and I was not coming back there. I told him I will call him later that I had to leave and one thing I did not tell him is about the checks that I received or the ones that she is going to give me. He looked at me and said ok I understand and I gave him a kiss and I walked out the door. He said to call him and let him know what was going on when I get myself settled in. I left and I did not look back for nothing as if I would turn to a pillar of salt like in the Bible. Deep down inside I knew that it would be a long time before I saw him again. As I was walking to the train I stopped in my tracks and I turned around to go back to the building as I got closer I saw him leaning out the window probably watching me. A big smile came on his face when he saw me coming back, can you through the keys down please. I went upstairs and he was standing there with the door open and I walked inside and gave him the keys back. Did you forget something why did you come back did you change your mind? No I smiled I did not change my mind but I did forget something. I forgot to tell you thank you for all that you did for me especially when I was in Brooklyn and when I came home from the hospital. I don't want to leave without telling you that face to face I do really appreciate what you did for me. I want you to know that really I do and I could not leave without telling you that. He says you really want to punish me I thought for sure you had changed your mind and was coming back home.

Heading to the train back to Brooklyn where I have not been in four years since I left there in the middle of the night to move to Harlem. I wanted to turn around so many times instead of facing them at least in Harlem I did not have to answer to anyone about anything but I know I would die there too and I did not want that to happen. I know that was not the plan the God had for me I had to rely on Him and Him alone to get me through this. Will I be forgiven or will He turn His back on me and leave me out here all alone. I just prayed that they will be understanding and patient with me while I once again put my life in order. My daughter is having another baby her third one and I could not be happier for her. One thing I know about my children now that they have their own I don't have to worry about them taking good care of them. They don't want to put them through what they went through and I am so great full they turned out to be great parents.

As I sit on the train I can't help but to think about Danny I wish I could have seen him to say goodbye or give him a phone number or address for him to come and see me. I guess it was meant to be. Too bad I will never see him again well bye baby thanks for the memories.

Hi I am here I called her and she was at her mother's house who lives across the street from her how great is that. I am on my way right now wait right there don't go nowhere. We get upstairs and I begin to talk to her and with the tears running down my face. Your Son is on his way upstairs talk to him and let's see what we can do. Hi mama what's wrong why are you crying what happened? I started getting high again and I think I should go away this time so I don't hurt anyone else anymore. I am sorry for letting you down I don't want to be a burden on anyone. I left my job after I went and spoke to my boss and I told her what she already knew so I have to pick up a check. I will find a place to go to I will make some calls and see which one will be best for me. Ma wait you don't have to go anywhere just stay here with us and we will take it day by day one day at a time. I know you will be ok I just know you will I am not worried about that. But you do not have enough room so I have to find a place. There is room we will get a folding bed and put in the living room and your granddaughter wants you to stay so then it's settled.

Regardless of what I think God might think something else. I had to at least try and see if He would help me or if I just listen I might have a change for His Grace and Mercy and most of all His forgiveness. If given another opportunity I will know exactly what to do with it. I prayed hard and I do mean hard and sincere and that is what He is looking for in order to get an answer. Reading my Bible all the time and listening to my gospel CD's and most of all not thinking about that dam pipe.

I started to going over to my daughter's house to help her with my grandchildren since she was having another baby and thought that I could be of some help to her. I have to find a job and get some money coming in one thing is for sure that you cannot live anyplace for free I don't care if its family or not. Before I started looking for a job I went back to my old job and got the checks that she said I could come and get. Hi how are you everyone said when I got off the elevator and started walking towards my ex bosses office. Come in and she gave me a hug and said you look good girl healthy that is a great look on you have not seen that since you started working here very nice. Thank you I am staying with my kids and helping my daughter with my grandchildren she is having another baby. So are you in a program like you said that you would do? No I am not I told my kids that is what I was going to do and they said just take one day at a time stay away from negative people and places and pray you will be fine. If that does not work for you and you see yourself going back down the same road yes please we will get you the help you need. That is great to have family that you can depend on and who love you no matter what. Yes it is truly a blessing for sure. We talked for a while and I went out and spoke and laughed with some of the ladies working there who was very happy to see me and to see that I was looking good. I said my good byes and headed back to Brooklyn, it would have been easy to make a detour and head to Harlem but guess what I cannot let HIM down again. So I smiled as the train left Manhattan and headed to Brooklyn.

I started going out looking for a job and leaving my resume every place that I could and going on interviews. There was one job that I went to for an interview for a Customer Service position. This is far I told myself I hope they do not call me back I would not want to come way out her to go to work. Well guess what happened yes your right they called me back. Two weeks had passed and I got the call and he asked if I found a job yet and I now but I could not remember from his name which job he was calling from. When he said where he was calling from I was like dam but guess what I did not refuse the position I started that Monday.

Now you may say really she has been out of work for only two months and already she found a job I mean there are people that have been looking for a job for years and still have not found anything. Jesus came to save sinners and I am the biggest sinner of them all and He still loves me no matter what is that awesome or what. I did not want that job but God puts you where you need to be not where you want to be. I learned that about my God, His thoughts are not our thoughts and His thinking is different than the way we think. I serve an awesome God for sure. He has never let me down and I know for sure that Jesus is the only friend that I have and that's all the friend I need.

My daughter had a little girl and her too I trained her little but to go to the bathroom like I did her sister and brother. I stayed with my daughter for a long time for the first time since my accident and I was alive ready to do whatever. No I did not go back to the pipe although one time I tried to do it but I could not it never happened and I am glad that it did not real glad that was a Holy Ghost intervention. I would go out and party and drink I guess when you lose one habit you pick up another one that you think is not as bad as the first one but a habit is a habit and they are all bad.

I started my job and I went to work all the way out there in no man's land and I had great bosses and their mother worked there too. It was not long before it felt like I had been there so long I opened every morning I just knew I was important. After a while I did not care that I had to go so far it was worth it to have a job one that I liked. One day I was walking to work from the train and I saw this guy staring and smiling. I would smile back and keep on walking with y sexy walk that I had I just knew he was watching me as I walked pass. One day he decides to come off his mini bus and come speak to me. I watched you every day and I wanted so bad to speak to you but I was scared that you would not speak back or curse me out. You're not going to curse me out are you? Now

I am not going to curse you out why would I do that I will not do something like that unless you gave me a reason to?

Every day he would see me, and we would talk and then I gave him my number and he would call and come over to my daughter's house and spend the night sometimes. Things were going well and he made me very happy and I would not want to be with anyone else. He was funny and made me laugh. One day he came over and was getting ready to leave and he asked me to marry him. What the hell is wrong with you I said marry what are you talking about that is something you should not play with if you know what I mean. Baby I am serious I really want to marry you that is if you say yes. Ok where is my ring if you're asking me to marry you where is the ring. I will have it tomorrow when I come but after that I have to leave I found another job and I have to move. What another job and moving where so how are we going to get married I am not moving anywhere. Please I have to talk to you about something very important and I hope you understand. The next day he came over and I was not home he left the ring with my daughter which I feel was tacky but I took it. The weekend I went to meet him on upstate and I asked why can't you come here why do I have to leave and meet you. He said that he cannot leave from there it was part of the program he was in and that blew my mind. What program what the hell are you talking about are you a drug addict why didn't you tell me that I cannot be around anyone like that. I don't get high anymore I am clean and I have a good job and if you would move here we can get an apartment together I need you. Oh brother I needed someone too strong man not a weak one. If you looked at him you would not think that I had no clue. We talked and I went back to Brooklyn and yep I moved to Beacon, NY and was engaged to this man who at the time made me very happy. I met his family and I would cook thanksgiving dinner and they would come along with my family it was great but then he started acting funny. I move all the way up here and you want to get on my dam nerves you got to be crazy. I knew then that I was not going to stay with him had the nerve to tell me that I am too good a woman and I deserve to have someone that could love me the way I needed to be loved it was not him. And then the last straw I found out that he had another bitch on the side and that was it either I go to jail or I leave. I was sick and I got on the train and never returned to that apartment I asked that he pack my stuff and ship it to me I did not want to see him again. This is bull shit I was done back to Brooklyn I go at least I did not have to take the dam metro north. Free again and every man that I met after that were all the wrong men. The only man I ever loved was my Ronald and even to this day I wish I could see him again the love of my life and I never told him how much I really cared for him.

I did keep in touch with my ole man in Harlem and he had moved out of that apartment into a senior citizen home and a very nice one. We called on another and I would even go and visit him in and spend the night one time. My daughter would even go and see him if he needed something or if I needed something he would tell her to come over and she would go and take the grands to see him. One whole weekend I was trying to call him and got no answer and that was not like him not to return my call. Monday at work I called again but this time he answered but he could not speak it sounded like he had some sought of stroke I called right away his daughter and she called the ambulance. He was in Harlem Hospital and I went to see him after work and when I saw him my heart broke. He could not speak so he followed me with his eyes and I hugged him trying not to cry, he did not look good he had a stroke and he had been like that on the floor all weekend. It was time for me to go visiting hours was over and he looked at me as if to say please don't leave me. I have to go and I hugged him again and walked out as fast as I could so he would not see me crying. I would call his daughter every day to see how he was and I would go and see him on the weekend again. She called me that Saturday and told me I should come and see him he is not doing well. I will be there tomorrow but she called me back and told me that he was gone so I did not get the chance to say goodbye. Sad time no matter what I did love him in my own way and I know he loved me for sure.

He died March 20. 1999....... at the funeral I walked up to the coffin and he had a tear running down his right eye and it stopped a tear how is that possible a tear and it stopped that's all everyone could talk about. Why are you crying rest in peace I love you. Even after I left Harlem I still went to mu Church there for a while.

CHAPTER

14

All Is Well its 2015

December 31, 1999 and the world is going to end. Stores are empty of batteries and flashlights and people saying that 2000 years Jesus is coming back and everyone was praying at 11:59pm. Well there was no light in the sky no trumpets sounded and we are still alive. Well suppose Jesus said maybe I will wait until it gets light outside and then make it dark and return no one knew for sure.

Well we are all still alive thank God and I am still at the same job believe it or not and all is well. Now the partying and everything I still did every Friday when I got home I would go and get me six pack corona and a bottle and make my drinks put on some music and dance with my grands for a while and hit the road. Besides all the hanging out I had asthma and when I got sick with a cold I would wind up in the emergency room and then being admitted to the hospital but that did not stop me from smoking cigarettes. Until one time I was very sick and was admitted to the hospital and this was the worst attack I had and got home and wanted a cigarette. Now I had been promising God that I would stop smoking every time I had an asthma attack. But I never did but this last time I begged my daughter go get me one cigarette and she did. Listen people because what I am about to tell you is the honest truth. While I was begging my daughter to buy me one a voice said don't do it I will take your breath away if you think I am playing. Well that voice came and went and I got that cigarette and lite it and took a pull when I say I could not breath. I heard that same voice say you think I am playing with you and I had tears running down my face it was as if I was taking my last breath. My daughter was crying and when I was able to catch my breath I threw that cigarette down with tears in my eyes I said I believe you. That was my last cigarette going on ten years now cannot pay me to touch a cigarette cannot stand to be around it.

The year 2000 came in and Rosalind has been doing pretty well. Had a couple of major surgeries and thank God they all went well. This is including a total hip replacement which is something that I never thought would happen ever. The men in her life well there are no men in her life. She has not found that special someone and just when she thought she did he turned out to be a jerk. Single and looking one thing she learned and that is if he doesn't want you don't make him think he does, he never will. Find someone that will love you for you and accept the fact that if it does not happen oh well. But that's a lie we all need to be loved and told how special we are. I miss that not having anyone special to hold me when I cry and to tell me it's ok that our love will overcome all. I have never been told that yet but I am waiting.

Anyone who drinks mostly smokes so no cigarettes no drinking. See God felt that I did not need a crutch he took everything else away from me I don't need that either. And I will obey Him still because "To fear the Lord is the beginning of knowledge but fools despise wisdom and instruction".

Over the years I have grown and have become more dependent on my Lord then I have ever been. My life is not great I don't have a big house and many friends. I have no friends and no one to call my own. I am still at the same job for 19 years now I mean that is great for me I never thought that this is where I will be all these years later. Thank God I am still here and healthy still got issues that I deal with on a daily basis but nothing like what I have dealt with. My past is my past it does not identify who I am now. It takes time to mature and learn to love yourself more and more each day.

I am happy do I want to be happier of course I do. Will I be I am sure about that it's written already. I am successful because I have overcome a lot of things that most people do not come out on top. I know that someone reading this is going to thing that this did not happen she is making this up. How can someone go through all this and still be alive. That's when you learn that when I could not walk someone was carrying me. It's a spiritual thing I cannot explain it but its real something you feel in your spirit. I dare you to try Him for yourself just give Him a chance you will not be disappointed.

It's 2015 and I and I now have 7 grandchildren and 2 great grands and after a lot of moving I am back with my daughter. I love my grands and my daughter has 4 kids 2 girls and 2 boys and my son has 3 daughters. I could not be happier to have them in my life I am great full and blessed. My sister and brother are well thank God. Oh wait my mother who is now 89 years young is doing well great to still have her here with us.

At the end of this book I have poetry that I wrote pertaining to the life that I was living and events that happened in my life. I hope you will enjoy them and they will bless and touch you in a certain way no matter what you're going through. This book was written to be an inspiration to someone who is going through something and you may think that you cannot come out of it. But I am here to tell you that the devil is a liar and there is no truth in him. I wrote this book because Rosalind is real just like you and me and her story is too.

Dear Lord, I ask that whomever hands might touch this book and begin to read through the pages let them find the peace as I did. Let them see that no matter what he or she is going through there is nothing too hard for you. Change their lives and reach their hearts and minds as they look to you for change. What you did for me you can do the same for them I ask in Jesus Name. Amen

The following poems were written by me and I would like to take this time to say thank you for even looking at the cover of this book and then you opened it and I am forever grateful. These are a collection of some of my poetry and it reflects my life past and present.

As you read I pray that this will inspire someone if only the fact that you read it that will make a change in your life. Perhaps you will think about it making a change and I pray that Our Lord and Savior will guide you to a place of understanding and wholeness. May you be forever Blessed. This book was written with you in mind and by the guidance of the Holy Spirit.

Where Were You?

Where were you, that day when everything seemed wrong?
Where were you, I thought for sure our love was strong?
Where were you when I got the bad news?
Where were you, when I thought all I would lose?
Where were you, when your son was born?
You were nowhere a round to toot your own horn.
Where were you when he said his first word?
Somebody else told you, that's what I heard.
Where were you when he kept falling and getting up?
Where were you when he drank out of his first cup?
Where were you when he said do I have a dad?
Where the hell were you? I was so mad.
Well he is older now and no longer a child,
Don't have a good thing to say and that's putting it mild.
But this I will tell you and its coming from my heart,
I have your picture on the wall at that I throw darts.
Don't think for one minute that you're a father,
As a matter of fact oh what the hell, don't even bother.
You're not worth his time not in my book,
If you think you're a man then take a second look.
That's not a problem my son has a real man in his life,
He's an excellent father, because now I am someone's wife.
And oh yes he is very happy that's the father he knows,
He is very happy and in his eyes it shows.
So I just want to thank you for not being here,
God has blessed me, we don't need you my dear.
I thank God that I was able to call His name,
It's not your fault for God said not to blame.
For once in my life I found real love,
And I get all I need from the Man Above.

Be Blessed
Written by: Charlene McRae

What if?

What if, I were you and you were me?
What if what you thought is not what you see?
What if your family was not really yours?
What if your life was just one big chore?
What if you got up in another house?
What if your thoughts were as quiet as a mouse?
What if you looked in the mirror and your face you did not see?
What if I really wasn't me?
What if your black skin was white?
What if now you're short what happened to your height?
What if you went to work and they tell you that you're in the wrong place?
What would you do in that case?
What if no one knows you at all?
What if is your name or do you recall?
What if your mother was no longer there?
What if you're crazy and on one to care?
What if you find out that you have a different name?
What if you find out that nothing is the same?
What if you're dreaming and you want to wake up?
What if you're not and here you are stuck?
What if I tell you that it will be ok?
What if I tell you sorry life's just that way?
What will you say?

Be Blessed
Written by Charlene McRae

Through A Childs Eyes

Look Daddy as his little girl pointed to the sky,
Look how high those birds can fly.
How high Daddy do you think they can go?
He looks with amazement and say's I really don't know.
Look at the flowers daddy how do they turn to red?
Once again he looks at her and begins to rub his head.
Oh Daddy look at that, why is the tree so tall?
With all her questions he is running into a blank wall.
As he sat on the bench to watch his daughter play,
He thought about all her questions and what he should say.
Daddy every minute, look at this and look at that,
There he looks in amazement while on the bench he sat.
She ran over to the bench and ran into his arms,
And right at that moment he remembered the book of Psalm.
Wow that is strange I don't even read the word,
I remember that book, from my grandmother I heard.
She must have been tired with all the running around,
She laid back in his arms without making a sound.
As he sat staring and he was almost in a daze,
He looked in one direction and stared with such glaze.
Thinking about all the questions that was running through his head,
And he had to come up with answers before putting his daughter
to bed.
Psalms that book for some reason I keep hearing in my mind,
I have to go home and read it, there is something I have to find.
After sitting for a while he picks up his little girl and takes a real
long look,
I have to go home now find the Bible and read some of that book.
After reaching home and of course now she is wide awake,
I don't want to give the wrong answers sounding like a fake.
My little princess do you mind if daddy reads a book,
No daddy I will play and he gave her that special look.
Oh here it is the book he had not seen for so long,

After his wife died it seemed like everything went wrong.
He looks through the index to find what page the book was on,
He sees an envelope with his wife's handwriting oh I wonder how long.
He wonders how long it was there and what could it be,
It has my name on it, his heart starting beating as he took a look to see.
Tears starting flowing and his hands began to shake,
Just to think that she wrote this I may not be able to take.
As he read the letter the tears began to cloud the words,
He had to stop a couple of times, because her voice is all he heard.
Be well my love and I know you don't read this book,
I don't mean to bring memories back but I am glad you took a look.
This wonderful book you hold in your hands has so much meaning for you,
It will get you through your lost and help with our daughter too.
I know you're a wonderful Dad and filling her with cheer,
That I know about you, something I hold so dear.
If you need to pray about something specific than Psalm is the book for you,
If you need wisdom and understanding, then Proverbs can help with that too.
I promise if you read this it will fill you with so much joy,
Don't be surprised if sometimes you feel like a little boy.
That is something that God does when you come to him with a good heart,
He will nourish and build you up and He does that so from Him you will never part.
Always remember that He can change your very life,
And answer the questions you might have as to why He took your wife.
Don't worry and don't be sad for remember I will always love you,
And I know that with our daughter and God that He will bring you through.
After reading the letter he had a big smile of his face,
Before he was sad, now joy took its place.
It's like she is here she knew here I would look,

I am so happy now that I finally found this book.
Later while putting his daughter to bed,
He kept hearing his wife's voice in his head.
Honey, guess what I think I can answer you now,
With the Bible in his hand he knew God would show him how.
From that day on he read the Bible every single day,
And now my daughter and I never forget to pray.

Be Blessed
Written By Charlene McRae

Someone

I know there is someone reading this and they are going through,
Walking around and don't really know what to do.
It could be your job that's getting you down,
Maybe it's that your children's father is not around.
Could be that you tried and all tried out,
Starting to wonder what is this life really about.
What about my tears I cry late at night when no one is around,
What about all my fake smiles that are really frowns?
What about all the honey you ok is there something I can do,
Can I help you with the kids or maybe watch them for you.
You need to get out girl and go find yourself a man,
If they only knew that is not even in my plans.
I want to scream out and yell can no body see,
All the pain I am feeling inside of me.
I thought you knew me but I see that you don't,
I am trying to tell you but I know that I won't.
The kids the job is not all that's on my mind,
I am searching and searching and I have yet to find,
I need something that only the powerful can give,
I need a reason a real reason to live.
Don't get me wrong I love my kids so much,
But here lately them I don't even touch.
Hi mommy is something wrong why you look so sad,
Did I do something am I the reason you're mad?
No baby no way that mommy is mad at you,
There is nothing in the world bad that you can do.
I am ok don't you worry about a thing,
Just remember to me so much joy that you bring.
Go change your clothes and get ready for a snack,
Oh God my chest hurts so bad hope it's not a heart attack.
Oh God this hurts please let this pain go away,
I have my children to think about please let me stay.
Be quiet now and be very still,
I will take the pain away because it is my will.

While I have you quiet let me say this to you,
I see your pain and I know what you're going through.
I have been here all the time but we never talk,
How is that pain doing are you able to walk.
Come have a seat and give me a minute,
I just want you to know I have always been in it.
What I mean by that is I am the Truth and The Light,
Let me be your friend and I can make everything right.
Before you go to bed tonight sit down and talk to me,
I can make it better just wait and see.
Tears began to flow and the pain was all gone,
I believe in that minute I was reborn.
That was a miracle it may seem little to some,
But after that I have already overcome.
Gone is the pain the doubt and the fear,
Here to stay is Jesus whom I hold so near.
Now when I smile it's not just for show,
I found the Savior so inside and out I glow.
To anyone who reads this you're not alone,
Jesus on the main line, just pick up the phone.

Be Blessed.
By Charlene McRae

Next

Next time I will do the things that really matter to me,
Next time I will open my eyes wide so that I may see.
Next time my heart will be open to new and exciting things,
Next time I will not hold out I will spread my wings.
Next time I will look in the mirror and see the real me,
Next time I will not get emotional I will just let things be.
Next time I feel something for the opposite sex,
Next time I won't have to put my feelings in a text.
Next time my dream seem to go up in smoke,
Next time I will be financially stable, I won't be broke.
Next time I will not let you bring me down,
Next time I will be strong enough to hold my ground.
Next time always seems to be a good word to say,
Next time may not come what will you do that day?
Next time sounds good so get your fill,
Next time is yours if it is God's will.

Be Blessed
Written by Charlene McRae

Are You?

Are you a dreamer just dream all the day?
Are you a dreamer come, what may?
Are you the type to do what has to be done?
Are you that someone who says how you doing hun?
Are you the one that appeared in my dream?
Are you the one that I will want on my team?
Are you the one who holds the key to my heart?
Are you the one that will fall apart?
Are you that special someone from above?
Are you that someone that I should love?
Are you the one that will hold me real tight?
Are you the one that I will kiss goodnight?
Are you the one who if apart I feel I would die?
Are you the one who will make me cry?
Are you that someone that can see the real me?
Are you the one that will set me free?
Are you someone I want to be with will you make me your wife?
Oh never mind Jesus has all that I want I will be with Him for the
rest of my life.

Be Blessed
Written by Charlene McRae

Looking For Me?

How often do you take time just for you?
Is there something special that you can do?
When was the last time you had a smile on your face?
When was the last time you were in a good place?
When was the last time you wore that sexy dress?
Without doing it for someone you were trying to impress.
Where is that girl who was always ahead of the game?
When it was not all about the fortune and fame.
Where is that head you use to have on your shoulders?
The one without fear and you became bolder.
Take a step back and look real good,
You're the same one that came from the hood,
Yeah you remember how you used to be,
But do you remember what it felt like to be free?
Look over the mountain and down the hills,
Look at your wallet the money that pays your bills.
You don't have to look far for the answer is plain to see,
The person I'm looking for is me!

Be Blessed
Written By Charlene McRae

How You Doing?

How do you like your meat rare or well done?
How do you like parks? Do you think their fun?
How do you feel when someone cries?
How do you feel when something dies?
How do you like yourself good or bad?
How do you see yourself happy or sad?
How about your life are you a success?
Or is your life a total mess?
How is your family does everyone get along?
Or does someone have another tune to that song.
Well how about your job are you happy there?
Or are you looking to work elsewhere.
How do you like your man tall and fine?
Or someone to say the he is mine.
I respect your answer whatever it may be,
But I only have one answer but that's just for me.
No matter how fine no matter how tall,
No matter my job that means nothing at all.
No matter that dress for it's just something to wear,
No matter that look stay with me if you dare.
No matter my problems I have something for that,
No matter my face that always looks back.
There is only one thing that matters to me,
Am I going to Heaven for Jesus face I long to see.

Be Blessed
Written By Charlene McRae

Prayer

What happens when you can no longer find you way,
What happens when you run out of words to say?
What happens when there is no place left to turn?
What happens when your heart no longer yearns?
Is there someone that can come and save the day?
Is there someone that perhaps you should pray?
I know some of you are all prayed out,
Feel that there is nothing left to shout about.
Well now look real good go way down deep,
I mean search your soul and take a peek.
Now if you can remember the last time you called,
And remember the one who is able to do it all.
You have to remember who you're talking to,
You have to ask and believe if you want Him to answer you.
Now if you need an answer and you need it right away,
GOD can perform miracles without any delays.
I have a testimony and I promise this is true,
What He did for me He will do the same for you.
The life that I have now is because of Him,
Believe me there was a time my life was very grim.
If you want to see a miracle just take a good look at me,
You would not believe how I was before He set me free.
If you think that your life is not worth saving,
Then come talk to me I will show you how I was behaving.
But Glory Be to God for my sins I was forgiven,
I am a miracle you should see now how I'm liven.
Humble yourself before Him and put in your request,
Be careful what you ask for you He will test.
Don't try and be fancy using words you don't need,
Ask the Holy Spirit to come and the words He will feed.
Now once you ask and you leave everything to Him,
Don't start worrying and make the light in your spirit go dim.

Take it to the Lord and leave it there and in time you'll see,
Everything asked in Faith it will surely be.
Always remember that He will take care of you,
There is nothing you can ask for that God cannot do.
So go ahead get up now and go on your way,
And while you're at it Have a Blessed Day!

In Jesus Name
Amen.

Be Blessed
Written by Charlene McRae

Love

That is one word that means so much,
It's so powerful you feel it with one touch.
Love can be good and love can be bad,
Love can make you lose all that you had.
Love is soft and gentle and kind,
Love is something you search hard to find.
Love is felt by children too,
But so often it gets them confused.
You see if you love me don't bring me pain,
For in that kind of love there is nothing to gain.
Love me the way that puts a smile on my face,
Anything else would be a disgrace.
Love is not a black eye I don't need you for that,
Love is not looking in the mirror and seeing my lip fat.
Back up for a minute do you need to know what love is?
Well, let me tell you and it goes something like this.
Today I woke up feeling all brand new,
Feeling this way and it's all because of you.
You were beside me in my bed when I went to sleep,
But before I did you made me yours to keep.
You told me you loved me with all your heart,
There was nothing in this world that can keep us apart.
I got butterflies in my belly feeling like a child,
Your kiss was so gentle tender and mild.
You woke every feeling inside of me,
And I felt the same way for a long time you see.
Finally it happened the love of my life,
Now I will finally be someone's wife.
For all you ladies that want this kind man,
Just be yourself and hold on if you can.
There is someone out there that can make you smile,
But sometimes it just might take a while.
But don't give up and keep your ways,
Don't give in not even for a day.

If he don't make you feel like a little girl,
Then trust me Sista don't let him in your world.
Stick to your guns and say a little pray,
God will send you someone that really cares.
I know it's been a long time but listen to me,
Although I'm still single I love being free.
But I'm not going to lie sometimes I get lonely,
But I'd rather wait then deal with a phony.
When you find love you will be the first to know,
Everyone will know when they see that glow.

Be Blessed
Written By Charlene McRae

I Miss You...

I don't understand something has to be done,
I think there was a little mix up and you called the wrong one.
She is sweet and kind was always there for me,
I don't have the answer but this could not be.
Please forgive me God, I am not saying why,
Because I know for sure we all have to die.
But why her why now I don't know what else to say,
I just wish I could have her for a couple more days.
If it's ok I need a favor, I know you have a lot to do,
But if it's ok I would like to put in a word or two.
I know you already met her and she had a big smile on her face,
And I want her to know in me she left a trace.
Tell her I miss her and another I will never find,
And tell her how much I love her if you would be so kind.
There's just one last thing before I go,
With you she is happy and this I know.
Now when I look towards Heaven she is smiling at me,
I know in my heart her again I will see.
May God forever bless you and heal your heart,
Because the love she had for you that will never part.

Be Blessed.
Written by Charlene McRae

I Know Him by Name

I know Him by name he has a very sweet voice,
He helps me all the time to make the right choice.
There was a time when I was dead,
His name and His voice they were not in my head.
I knew His name then but I did not care,
Me, call on His name I would not dare.
Don't call on Him you have to stay with me,
I will make you feel good and there's a lot you will see.
Like a fool I listened to that other voice,
For so many years I made the wrong choice.
I passed by a mirror and what did I see,
I saw someone but it sure didn't look like me.
It was horrible I looked like hell,
I had the same name that was all I could tell.
Well time went on and I could not break free,
The grip was tight and my eyes could no longer see.
Drugs and drinks took over all that I had,
It's like it didn't even matter and that's what was bad.
All was gone my life and my kids,
Felt almost like I was doing a bid.
Well yes I was in a prison called hell,
And the one with the key he knew me so well.
It was one of those days with my drugs on the table,
Not knowing that Jesus was still willing and able.
Something came over me I cannot explain,
I wondered what will happen if I just called His name.
Oh He will not answer look at the wrong you've done,
Probably can't call on God or His Son.
Then I thought back when I was a member in His house,
Call on the Lord He will help without a doubt.
Jesus it's me I hope you remember my voice,
I have decided to make you my choice.
Please hear me Lord for I am buried deep in sin,

And give me a chance to start all over again.
Tears flowing down I didn't know what to say,
With my eyes towards Heaven I began to pray.
So I prayed from my soul through all the hurt and the pain,
I prayed until the tears came down like rain.
With His strong arm He reached down and took my hand,
I am here my child I will make it so you can stand.
Thank you Jesus for you cleaned me up and turned me around,
Put my feet on solid ground.
I am alive and no longer living in sin,
Praise God for His Son Jesus for my soul He did win.

Be Blessed
Written by Charlene McRae

Funny

Funny how we sometimes forget who we are,
You let others shape you and you look from afar.
You begin to remember who that is you see,
Why don't they just let you be?
But that's your fault stop living for others,
Don't take it from your sister or brother.
You have a life one that no one can take,
But if you allow it then you become a fake.
Hold your head up and be proud and strong,
You don't need someone else to belong.
God gave life to you and that you must live,
Be the best you can and remember to give.
Give of yourself be a guiding light,
And put your hands up and learn how to fight.
Fight for your life and know you must win,
No matter what the circumstance no matter the kin.
If you don't love yourself no one else will,
Take your life back and get your fill.
Ask for strength that comes from above,
Remember God loves you He doesn't push or shove.
He gently takes you under his wings,
You sour to new heights and see all wonderful things.
Don't worry about a thing He has your back,
If you feel like your falling He will put you on the right track.
Be Strong Be Prayerful At All Times!!

Be Blessed
Written By Charlene McRae

Do You Know Him?

Praise Him all the earth shall sing praises to the King,
Let everything that has a voice sing out let it ring.
As you go through your day take a minute and say,
Thank you Lord and then you began to pray.
Praise Him, the One who sits high and looks low,
Praise Him and watch the blessing flow.
All the pain He suffered just for our sins,
It is because of Him we can smile not just grin.
Don't take it lightly as some of us do,
He did it so that God can pardon you.
All your sins that you have and for you He died,
It is written in God's word and for sure He never lied.
Beaten whipped pierced in His side,
Are you going to now try to run and hide?
If you don't know His word than just pick up His book,
I am telling you now it is worth the look.
Greatest book in the world the New & the Old,
Just like the movie "The Greatest Story Ever Told".
Read the Old Testament and see all the good that He has done,
Then go to the New Testament and read all about His Son.
If there is something that you don't understand,
Don't get discouraged just ask Him to take your hand.
The Holy Spirit will come and help you to know,
Oh yes He will help so the words begin to flow.
Oh my God it seems like your talking to me,
Oh yes that happens a lot just keep reading and you'll see.
A book that was written so long ago,
How in the world can this feeling be so?
Well dear one from the beginning of time God had you in mind,
No matter how old you are He still hopes it's Him you will find.
If something happened in your life and you're wondering why,
Why am I still here why didn't I die?

Then look up to Heaven and say oh now I see,
That was you all the time watching over me.
Seek the Lord and you shall find Him,
He is the light of the world and His light never goes dim.
I pray that in your search you will find,
The One True Living God that will give you peace of mind.
There's just one more thing that I will like to say,
Just don't cease searching for Him and He will light your way.

Be Blessed
Written By: Charlene McRae

"Smile"

What is the cost to put a smile on your face?
What does it mean to the whole human race?

How does it feel to walk with a frown?
It's just a smile turned upside down.

See that's the problem with the world today,
No one has anything nice to say.

People are so busy running to and fro,
And not really having no place to go.

Do yourself a favor and follow my lead,
It is still not too late to take heed.

Listen to me and you can't go wrong,
It's something to do and it doesn't take long.

When you wake in the morning put a smile on your face,
And all through the day please don't erase.

And the next thing you know you will smile all the time.
And finally that frown will be left behind.

HAPPY SMILES DAY
Written by CHARLENE MCRAE

www.ingramcontent.com/pod-product-compliance
Lightning Source LLC
Chambersburg PA
CBHW022112050726
47591CB00002B/773